Murder at Christmas in Honeysuckle Grove

Denise Jaden

Copyright

MURDER AT CHRISTMAS IN HONEYSUCKLE GROVE (A MALLORY BECK AND TABITHA CHASE MYSTERY)

First Edition. November, 2023.

Copyright © 2023 Denise Jaden

Written by Denise Jaden

Join my mystery readers' newsletter today!

Sign up now, and you'll get access to a special mystery to accompany this series—an exclusive bonus for newsletter subscribers. In addition, you'll be the first to hear about new releases and sales, and receive special excerpts and behind-the-scenes bonuses.

Visit the link below to sign up and receive your bonus mystery:

https://www.subscribepage.com/mysterysignup

Murder at Christmas in Honeysuckle Grove

TABBY'S FAMILY HAS BUSY Christmas plans, which gives her the opportunity to fly across the country and visit West Virginia for the first time. Mallory and Amber both welcome Tabby to Honeysuckle Grove with open arms, but Hunch? He's not so sure about a woman who unmistakably smells of another cat.

They settle in to celebrate the holidays together, and when Mallory and Tabby open Christmas gifts from under the tree and find an item that has no discernible benefactor, trying to discover its origin and purpose becomes the number one task on their Christmas agenda. Is it a treasure hunt constructed by Amber? Or Alex? Or both of them?

While they search for clues, Mallory prepares for an upcoming catering event. The mysterious gift's source doesn't become evident until a couple days later when Mallory's and Amber's catering event turns deadly!

If you've enjoyed the Mallory Beck Cozy Culinary Capers or the Tabitha Chase Days of the Week Mysteries, you'll love this whodunit where the sleuths team up to solve an unforgettable case.

Chapter One - Tabby

I WASN'T SURE IF I was nervous or excited as I made my way from baggage claim to the airport exit. I hadn't seen Mallory or Amber in almost a year, and I had only met them in person during their one visit to Crystal Cove. What if I didn't even recognize them?

We had been emailing for months, of course—at least Mallory and I had—so we weren't strangers. But I had never been to the east coast, certainly never to West Virginia, and a big part of me still couldn't believe I had so quickly accepted Mallory's invitation to visit for Christmas.

But my sister Pepper would be working long hours over the holidays at the Crystal Cove hospital back in Oregon and my parents had decided to visit Europe for the first time. Pepper wanted to stay on my houseboat where she'd have my cat Sherlock for company so there had been nothing stopping me. I still couldn't get over the fact that my workaholic senator-dad was taking an actual vacation.

I was lost in thought and almost missed the two females frantically waving in my direction. As soon as I set eyes on them, recognition hit. They looked exactly the same as when I'd met them last April, except Mallory's dark hair now hung a few inches longer, to her mid back, while Amber's auburn hair had been chopped ultra-short. She wore a bright green hoodie that read:

TODAY'S PLANS:

1. HAVE FUN

2. DON'T DIE

I grinned and dragged my wheeled suitcase straight for them. I had borrowed an extra-large suitcase from my boss at the café, as not only had I packed Christmas gifts for my hosts, I had to include all the warm clothes I owned. In Crystal Cove, Oregon we rarely got more than a small smattering of snowfall, but Mallory had forewarned me that I could expect a very white Christmas at her house.

"I'm so glad you could make it." Mallory came in for a hug, and she instantly felt like a close friend I'd known my whole life. "Too bad Jay couldn't come," she said as she released me.

"Jay could have hung out with Mallory's boyfriend Alex," Amber put in.

Mallory's cheeks flushed, as I'm sure did mine. Jay and I had grown close, but it had taken us over a year to go on an actual date. I was certain it would be a decade before we were taking vacations together.

"I mean, they're both detectives," Amber went on. I didn't know if she was trying to relieve Mallory's shyness or mine over the subject, or if she just felt the need to explain further.

"Jay will be swamped through the holidays," I explained. "Ever since he took the place of our Senior Detective, it's nearly impossible for him to find time for even a single day off."

Amber grabbed for my suitcase handle and started to wheel it toward the exit.

"Oh, I can..." but I trailed off, because she was already out of earshot.

"Don't worry, I know where she parked." Mallory winked as we followed Amber at a distance.

"She drove?"

Mallory nodded. "She loves driving, and even though I feel a bit of reluctance when the snow is so heavy, she really is a good driver. Probably better than me. We brought the catering van, as it does better than my little car in this kind of weather."

I had heard all about their catering van and was excited to get to ride inside it. But when we made it through the parking lot and it came into view, Amber was slamming the back door on my suitcase, and it was immediately apparent that the front cab looked like your average vehicle.

I opened my mouth to ask if I could see inside the back, but Amber was already headed for the driver's seat. Mallory said, "It's about an hour to my place, so feel free to have a little nap on the way."

The van cab contained one bench seat, so it was doubtful that would happen. I told her, "I actually slept quite well on the plane. Besides, I've never been to this part of the country and I'm excited to see it."

Amber rolled her eyes as she said, "All you're going to see this time of year is white on top of white. I hope you brought sunglasses."

I produced a pair out of my purse while Mallory took the center seat and I got into the passenger one. As we drove out of the parking garage, Mallory directed Amber, but Amber said, "Calm down, Mom. My GPS is already hooked up."

I loved the easy relationship between these two. It definitely wasn't like mother and daughter. Closer to the relationship Pepper and I'd had as teenagers. As they chattered on, filling every second of dead space, I relaxed back into my seat, gazing out the window at the unfamiliar landscape of flat land and stretched-out highways. Most of their conversation came out like an argument, but I already knew them well enough to understand they weren't truly arguing. They were just being themselves with each other. They weren't afraid of the other getting offended and leaving. There was an importance between them that almost made me a little jealous.

"She hasn't been here before," Amber went on and I clued back into their conversation/argument, realizing it was about me. "We should definitely pick up a grape and gorgonzola pie."

"I'm making her something more interesting than pizza at the house," Mallory said. "I just went shopping and I've had a pot roast simmering all morning."

Amber rolled her eyes. "You'll just want to make her biscuits and gravy or something boring."

"You ladies are making me hungry," I said, chuckling.

"See?" Amber said, only looking away from the road for a half a second. She really did seem comfortable behind the wheel. "We should at least stop and get her a pepperoni roll."

Mallory conceded, and I wasn't sure about the sound of a pepperoni roll, but Mallory was a chef and she'd been teaching Amber to cook for over a year, so I trusted them when it came to cuisine.

Without being directed, Amber took the next exit. I was pretty tired and achy from the flight and in all honesty just wanted to get back to Mallory's house. But if these two had come to an agreement about anything, I probably shouldn't get in the middle and start them arguing again.

I expected Amber to pull up to a restaurant and was surprised when she instead pulled up to a minimart called the Frontier General Store. Amber opened the driver's door, and before I could reach for mine, Mallory popped out on the driver's side and said, "I'll just be two shakes. Stay warm inside."

Amber left the heat running, and Mallory was back quickly with three pepperoni rolls that, I had to admit, smelled absolutely amazing.

She passed the first one to me. "Now they're not very big, but they are filling, so I only got you one. I'm making you dinner at home so I don't want to ruin your appetite."

They weren't huge, that was true, but my first bite into the crispy bun and spicy meat was a real treat for my mouth.

If this was takeout, and only my first experience with food on this trip, I was eager to see—or taste—what the rest of my trip would hold.

Soon we headed up into the mountains, and the time passed quickly with me telling them about my family's plans for Christmas and them explaining how Amber had gotten an internship with the local police department during her breaks from college where she was studying forensic science. She had been looking at colleges on the West Coast when she'd visited Crystal Cove, but I guessed the internship had given her a reason to stick close to home. She would be working on Christmas Eve and Christmas Day, so the two of them planned to cook for me tonight and tomorrow morning.

When Amber took the exit into Honeysuckle Grove, the colored Christmas lights lit up buildings against a mountainous snowy backdrop. It was after six and the sun had set. The architecture was such a contrast to Oregon—many colonial-type buildings and, as we made our way from the town center, several log cabins came into view as well. While Mallory's house seemed to be beautiful-yet-average as we arrived at it, it was more sprawling than the suburban houses in either Crystal Cove or Portland, with plenty of land surrounding it.

After Amber parked, I headed for the rear of the van for my suitcase. Mallory opened the back door and I asked, "Any chance I can have a peek inside?"

Amber scoffed. "If you want to look at plain stainless-steel counters and pretty much nothing else, go for it. You'll enjoy it more when we're actually using it on the 26th."

I looked to Mallory, but before I could form a question, she answered it.

"I was going to tell you... and I really hope you don't mind. We got a last-minute booking to cater a party for the family of one of Amber's friends on the 26th."

"Not my friend," Amber said, sounding a little indignant.

Mallory rolled her eyes. "Sorry, one of Amber's former high-school classmates. The Petersons have a party at their mansion every year. It'll be a great opportunity to get our catering business in front of an upper-class clientele. This is the first one they've asked us to cater."

Amber shrugged a shoulder, and a look of distaste came over her face. "Cindra Peterson's a snob if you ask me."

Mallory went on as if Amber hadn't spoken. "You totally don't have to come if you'd rather relax, but if you're up for it, we thought it would be fun if you joined us."

"I'd love to!" I said, without even taking time to think about it. Not only would I get to hear about their great new catering business, but I'd also get to experience it.

"Too bad we don't have an espresso maker, or Tabby could really help us step up our game," Amber said.

I nibbled my lip to keep my smile at bay, because little did they know that they would have their own espresso maker after Christmas morning. It was packed snuggly in my luggage, and already wrapped in shiny blue Christmas wrap. "Yeah, too bad," I said, turning to my suitcase and hauling it out of the van to avoid them seeing the grin on my face.

Mallory led the way to her front door. The driveway and front walkway had been shoveled, but the thick blanket of snow over everything else made the neighborhood appear quaint and untouched. I followed, shivering at the crisp air that had to be a good ten degrees colder than Crystal Cove.

Just inside the door, we were greeted by a gray cat, taller and thinner than Sherlock, and with shorter fur. He looked like he had a permanent scowl on his face, if that was possible with a cat.

"Did you miss us, Hunchie?" Amber cooed, sweeping the cat off the floor and into her arms.

"That's my cat, Hunch," Mallory explained. "He's a great little sleuth, but doesn't have much patience for anybody except for Amber." She sounded a little forlorn and the way the cat just accepted how Amber had him curled up like a baby in her arms, I didn't doubt this was true.

Still, the part of me that missed my own cat made me move closer and say, "Hi, Hunch." I held out my hand for him to sniff it, and as soon as he got a whiff, he struggled to get out of Amber's arms to smell more. "He must smell Sherlock on me."

"Can you imagine getting both our cats working on a case together?"

Amber asked, stroking Hunch casually, as though she didn't notice his intense interest in my fingers.

"That would be a trip," Mallory agreed.

I attempted to bring my hand up and over Hunch's back to pet him, but he wrenched his neck to keep sniffing at my fingers, so I decided to just let him investigate the way he apparently did best.

When Mallory showed me to my room, Hunch stayed at a distance, but watched my every move.

"Come on, Amber. Let's let Tabby get settled. We can get the sides ready to go with my pot roast. I'm sure Tabby will be ready to eat by the time she's unpacked," Mallory said, leading Amber back down the stairs.

Surprisingly, she was correct. I'd felt stuffed after the pepperoni roll I ate on the drive, but traveling really did take a lot out of me and I was more than ready to eat again.

But having been left on my own for a few minutes, I decided to quickly get my gift under the Christmas tree while Mallory and Amber were preoccupied. I hoisted my suitcase onto the bed and lifted out the blue foil-wrapped gift, pleased to see it had traveled quite well.

While the two of them banged pots and pans and argued over whatever they were cooking in the kitchen, I tiptoed down the stairs, into the living room and slid the gift under the tree, which was lit up with tiny blue bulbs that matched my present perfectly.

It was a real tree, and someone must have missed the watering stand at the bottom because my knees got a little moist. There were two other gifts under the tree and for a second I doubted myself again over my choice of gift. Was it too much? Would Mallory and Amber feel bad if they hadn't gotten me anything?

But I shook off my questions when I saw Hunch out of the corner of my eye studying me. Or, rather, studying the gifts under the tree. I had no doubt the second I was out of the room he would be over here investigating.

And so I didn't waste another minute crouched at the bottom of the tree, especially when I heard Mallory headed for the base of the stairs and calling me to come for pot roast with all the West Virginia fixings.

Chapter Two - Mallory

BY CHRISTMAS EVE, I was extra glad I had invited Tabby for Christmas. Alex was so busy, he had yet to find time to come over and meet her, and because Alex was busy, that, by association, meant that Amber was busy, too. Having them both working in an official capacity with the police force and spending so much time at the police station together, it was hard not to feel left out.

"Just the two of us tonight?" Tabby asked, coming down the stairs after having a nap.

I nodded. "The police station is always busy over the holidays, and whenever it gets busy, they call Amber in to help."

Aside from my own loneliness, I was proud of that girl. Not only had she graduated early and launched into her college studies with fervor, she balanced her schedule flawlessly after Alex put her name in as an option for an intern at the local police station's forensics lab.

"The hope is that Alex and Amber will make it over for a quick dinner tomorrow night. We exchanged gifts last week when they both had a day off, but I hoped I'd get to see them both for a few minutes over Christmas."

Tabby nodded. "I completely understand. It's why I was eager to get away over the holidays. My sister will be busy at the hospital, and Jay, well, he's barely come up for a breath since Aaron was elected mayor and left a gaping hole on the police roster."

I had been making an effort to get to know some of the police officer's wives and girlfriends in town over the last few months, but that was always how it felt with them—like making an effort. Tabby was different. Conversations with her were effortless. Even Hunch was different with her. He wasn't friendly, exactly, but he was very interested, as though he had the innate sense that she had also had some success with investigating murders.

"Well, since it's just the two of us, I want you to open my gift now." I led the way toward the living room, lit up by the Christmas tree, giving it a homey feel. "Then I can show you how to use it."

I was excited to give her the same vegetable slicer that Amber had given me for my birthday. After having spent countless hours in culinary school slicing and dicing, all that came pretty naturally to me, but I had to admit, this slicer did things like spiralizing vegetables with barely a single touch. In truth, Amber used the slicer more than I did. She didn't have the patience to learn how to get her slices perfectly even, and the gizmo had really dressed up our catering events, so when she suggested getting one for Tabby for Christmas, I knew it was the perfect idea. Tabby would love using it at the café to dress up her sandwiches.

"Here. Open it." I couldn't contain my excitement. I'd always loved giving gifts.

She looked hesitant as she turned the red wrapping over in her hands. "Maybe you should open my gift first."

I wondered if she had trouble receiving gifts. From what I'd heard, she hadn't spent the last couple of Christmases with her family, so perhaps she was out of practice. I resisted the urge to roll my eyes, as I probably would have if Amber had been this nervous about opening a simple gift. I headed for the tree. "We can open them at the same time. Which one should I open first?"

Her forehead creased. "I, um." She pointed to the larger blue gift. "That one's from me."

I tilted my head at the two gifts remaining under the tree. When I had left to pick Tabby up at the airport yesterday, the vegetable slicer was the only gift here. I just assumed she had brought both of these, perhaps one for me and one for Amber.

Had Amber slipped another gift under the tree when she had been over? The other gift had silver wrapping and was small and rectangular. It looked like the size and shape that it could contain a piece of jewelry.

Was it from Alex?

Tabby interrupted my thoughts. "Maybe you should wait until Amber's here, too. It's for both of you." I started to put the blue box back, surprised at its heavy weight, but she said, "Oh, never mind. I want you to open it now."

With that decided, we both sat back into my living room couch and tore at our wrapping. While she studied the writing on the back of the slicer to try to figure out what it did, I blinked several times, barely believing my eyes.

"Tabby, this is too much."

She smiled warmly. "It's not. You invited me for Christmas. You've been feeding me like a queen. I wanted to get this for you and Amber so you can have your own specialty coffee any time you want." She pointed at the card, which held a separate envelope inside. "I also included some of my favorite recipes. Tomorrow morning, I'll show you how to use it, and I'm happy to make coffee at your catering event, too. But for now..." she held up the slicer. "I think I'm going to need your help with this."

I had her pack her slicer into her suitcase, clean and in the box. "I have the exact same one, so let's use mine."

In the kitchen, she let me natter on about the menu I was planning for the catering event while I taught her how to julienne carrots, parsnips, and beets, and then spiralize a large zucchini. At the same time, I pulled out my cast iron skillet to whip up a skillet cornbread that would go nicely with the maple ham I'd had cooking all day.

"This is going to be so colorful," Tabby said, as she grabbed for another beet to try with the slicer.

"That's the best part. I mean, the slicer is all about looks, really, but I thought you might enjoy using it at the café with your sandwiches."

"Olivia's going to give me a raise when she sees what I do with this next week," she said with a chuckle. "So who is that last gift from under the tree? A bonus gift from Amber?"

"That's what I was thinking. We had a spending limit between us, so this might be her tricky way of going over it." I pulled out my phone, displeased with this thought. Amber couldn't afford to spend extra money, not while she was in school and working at an unpaid internship.

Me: I found an extra little gift under the tree. Did you have anything to do with this?

By the time I'd slid the skillet into the oven I had a reply.

Amber: I have no idea what you're talking about.

The problem with texting was that a person could never really tell when sarcasm came into play.

Me: Our limit was thirty dollars, and I'm pretty sure that chef's hat you bought me was already more than thirty dollars.

I pulled out another skillet to fry up some of Tabby's freshly-sliced vegetables when my phone pinged again.

Amber: I dunno. Maybe it's from Alex.

My face flushed at the thought. Alex had already gotten me a painting from a local gallery that I'd loved when we'd walked by it. I knew it hadn't been cheap. Had he gotten me a piece of jewelry as well?

I resisted the urge to text him and ask, because if it was something special from him, I didn't want to have a conversation about it via text. But Tabby must have been able to tell it was continuing to weigh on me, because after we sat together and ate dinner, and while we were cleaning up, she asked a question that sounded like it had been on the tip of her tongue all evening.

"Are you sure there's no label on that silver gift?"

I dried my hands and headed back for the living room. Hunch was already in there, paws on either side of the small gift as he sniffed at it. I wondered if he'd been listening to our conversation. If only I could make him talk, because surely he had to know who it was from.

"Who's it from, Hunch?" I asked, regardless of his inability to answer me. Tabby gave me a strange look, so I picked it up and turned it over in my hands to divert from the oddity. But there was nothing written on any side of it. It felt like it could be heavier than a piece of jewelry, which was somewhat of a relief to me.

"I think you should open it," Tabby said. "I mean, if someone wanted to be here when you opened it, they would have added a label, right?"

I had a feeling it was only Tabby's eagerness to see what was inside that was making this argument. But I had to admit, I was equally as eager.

Still, I said, "Maybe I should check with Alex first?"

It wasn't a real argument, and Tabby must have known it. She reached out and took the small silver box from me, and before I knew what she was doing, she had pried a piece of scotch tape away from the bottom.

"It's expensive paper so you see, if we do this carefully, then you can always tape it back up once you know what's inside. I know if Jay had given me a small gift in this shape, it most definitely would have me a little freaked out—not because I wouldn't love it, but because we're just so...new. But maybe you and Alex are different," she added, almost as an afterthought.

But we weren't different. We were new, too, not because we hadn't admitted our feelings for each other and not because we hadn't wanted to be in a relationship for a long time, but mostly because Alex was quite busy and Amber needed our friendship, and it didn't provide for a lot of time alone together.

I took the box back from Tabby. If we were going to peek inside, I was going to be the one to take the reins on that. Then Alex could only blame me, if he was going to blame anyone.

There was a surprising amount of tape snippets around the thing, and it took me several minutes to carefully pry all of them loose. I couldn't imagine we'd be able to make the gift look untouched again, but I figured we'd gone too far now to turn back, and so I pried off the last swatch of tape and then carefully unfolded the paper.

I hadn't been wrong. As soon as the gift wrap was off, it was clearly a white oblong jewelry box. I sucked in a breath and removed the cover.

Tabby tilted her head, moving closer. "Is it some kind of vape pen?"

I picked up the cylindrical stainless-steel object. It had a band of wood grain around the middle and had some weight to it. I'd seen something similar before, in a kitchen I'd once worked in, but that one had been larger.

"I think it's actually a..." I gave the thing a twist, and sure enough, it twisted at the wood grain. I pulled off the capped end at the top, and even though it was empty of spice, there was a swatch of paper tucked inside. As I pulled it out and unfolded it, I explained. "I'm pretty sure it's a spice grinder."

Tabby took the grinder to inspect it while I read the short typewritten note.

THE TOWEL CLOSET ISN'T WHERE THIS BELONGS. TIME TO INVESTIGATE!

I suppressed a smile, wondering if this had been Alex's handiwork or Amber's.

Or perhaps they'd been in it together. Then I eyed Tabby. She'd said the gift wasn't from her, but could she have sneakily organized some kind of treasure hunt for me?

I shook my head at myself because she had not been here long enough to put something like that together.

"There are some yellowy remnants of something inside," she said, trading me for the note.

I gave the cylinder a sniff. "Smells like saffron."

"Saffron is expensive, right?" The way she studied the note, I had no doubt she was as mystified as I was.

"It makes sense why the grinder is so small." My mind whirred with everything about it that could be a clue. "This has to be the start of a treasure hunt."

"You think it's actually from Amber?" Tabby asked.

"If it's really not from you, it has to be from either Alex or Amber. They're pretty much the only ones who ever come into my house, and Alex has only been here once in the last month—the day we exchanged gifts with Amber."

"I swear I've never seen this before in my life." Tabby held up a hand as if she were on the witness stand. "So Amber had to have left it, but she says she didn't?" Tabby raised an eyebrow, clearly thinking that this was just silly teenage stretching of the truth.

But I knew Amber better. We were close in a way that couldn't be forged from simply hanging out together for a couple of years. We had shared a similar grief—me for my husband and her for her dad. If she had wrapped up the grinder and then played dumb about it, it was for a good reason. Maybe she thought I'd be lonely without her over Christmas.

I did miss her, but having Tabby here had certainly softened the blow of being without her and Alex over the holidays. I wondered if Amber had organized this before she knew Tabby was coming.

I twisted my lips, picking up the grinder and studying it. I pulled off the bottom cap and gave it a twist to see if there was any saffron left in the blades, but the turn was smooth and I looked inside to see there were no blades. It looked as though the whole mechanism had been removed. "I'll bet Alex and Amber organized this to keep me occupied over the holidays," I said in response to Tabby's suggestion.

"So where do we start?"

I tapped my chin. "Well, if a tiny spice grinder is the start of a treasure hunt, what could it mean?" I liked the idea of figuring this out with Tabby more and more by the minute.

Chapter Three - Tabby

STRANGE THAT AMBER WOULDN'T have admitted to the treasure hunt and told Mallory this was her first clue. Then again, I didn't know their relationship very well. Perhaps they were such good sleuths that they knew it would take a super cryptic puzzle to be able to stump one another.

"Where's your towel closet?" I asked. We couldn't ignore the mention of it in the note. Mallory led the way upstairs and opened a hall closet with stacks of neatly folded towels and sheets.

She took one out and shook it open, but nothing came out. I held out my hands for the towel and refolded it as she checked the next one. We soon got into a rhythm. As we neared the final towels on the bottom shelf, Mallory said, "Leave it to Amber to plant the next clue in the very last one."

Except there was no note in any of them.

"Let me just check the walls and shelves." She ran a hand along each shelf and the inside of the walls, but still, there was nothing.

"Do you keep towels in your bathroom cupboards?" I asked, after we had replaced everything in the hall closet.

She led the way as we checked both bathrooms, but still found nothing.

I followed Mallory to her kitchen, grabbing the spice grinder and the note on our way. She checked through her dish towels in a drawer, but found nothing.

"Where do you keep your spices?" That seemed like the next logical place to look for another clue.

She opened an upper cupboard and moved several spice jars of varying sizes and shapes aside. She pulled each one out, passing them to me so I could check all sides and the bottom of each one for further clues. But there was nothing.

She pulled over a stepstool and continued checking the upper shelves. When we came up empty, we both leaned back against her counters, thinking.

"By the weight, it seems like it's made from solid steel," I suggested. "I don't know, does that seem unusual to you?"

She shrugged. "Not really. I've seen these kinds of grinders before, and the weight helps to keep you from dropping it in a busy commercial kitchen."

"But would you find such a small one in a busy commercial kitchen?" I asked.

"No, you're right. All the ones I've seen before have been quite a bit bigger, even for something like saffron." Mallory tapped a finger against her mouth. "The color, that's the unusual part about saffron."

I was busy searching the spices we had laid out on the counter again. "You don't have saffron?"

She shook her head. "I've bought it in small amounts in powder form for specific recipes, but it's really best if you grind the strands down fresh when you're using it. I can't say I use saffron often enough to warrant having a special saffron grinder." She chuckled at this, but I was still looking through her other spices.

"What else is yellow like saffron?"

She opened the barrel of the grinder and fished her finger inside. "It's actually more orangey-red before it's ground. See?" She showed me a small strand that had been left behind. "Turmeric looks a little like it once it's ground up." She passed me a spice container with a green lid that was labeled "Turmeric."

I had already checked the outside of the bottle, but I checked it again and then opened the top and peeked inside. It was about half full. I gave the bottle a little shake to see if there was something hidden within the spice, but I couldn't see anything.

Mallory kept busy surveying the rest of her spice bottles. "Safflower is probably the closest to saffron's unground version, but I don't have any of that."

"Hmm," I said, finally giving up on the turmeric. "I don't know."

Mallory chuckled. "Come on, Tabby. I know you don't give up that easily." She opened cupboards around her kitchen and closed them again. She moved small appliances around on the counter and looked underneath them. I stood watching her. In truth, I hadn't given up, but I was wracking my brain, because I knew the clue had to be something smart. Something that would really cause us to think hard.

"Should we check the towel cupboards again?" I didn't know what else to suggest.

Mallory nodded slowly, and then bent to check among her stack of tea towels. When she didn't find anything there, she led the way back to the hall closet and left me to search it while she checked under all the bathroom counters one more time.

Sure enough, we both came up empty, and before we could figure anything else out, the oven dinged and we had more important things to think about, namely my grumbling stomach.

Chapter Four - Mallory

BY THE EARLY AFTERNOON of the 26th, Tabby and I still hadn't found a second clue on our treasure hunt, but we'd had fun searching together. Once the stores were open, we'd gone around town, visiting specialty food shops and kitchen stores, and talking to plenty of sales associates about everything they knew about rare spices and unusual grinders.

It turned out the grinders were not terribly rare, but they were expensive. Over fifty dollars for this size, which was the smallest size grinder. We even looked into a few towel storage units in the bathroom aisle of our local hardware store, but they didn't spark any ideas about what the note could mean.

I'd texted Alex with: **I'm assuming this treasure hunt is to keep us busy?**

The only response I received was a question mark, which again didn't help at all. I couldn't tell if he was being coy or if I should have been focusing on Amber for answers. But I'd heard through her quick texts that the police station was incredibly busy these days. I was eager for her to arrive at my house so I could ask her more—both about the busyness of the police station and the treasure hunt.

But it had given Tabby and me something fun to do in between shopping and preparing for our event at the Peterson's mansion.

"Can I use this bin for all the coffee supplies?" Tabby asked me, holding up a blue Rubbermaid container.

"You bet," I told her. "When you have everything together, just load it right into the catering van. As soon as Amber gets here, I'll stock the fridge and we can go."

As if she could hear me speaking her name, a text popped up on my phone screen at that moment.

Amber: OK if I meet you there? I got in late and just woke up.

After texting her back, telling her that was fine and that we already had almost everything packed, I turned to Tabby. "That's not like Amber, to sleep until the afternoon. In fact, when I first met her, she barely slept at all." I was relieved she was sleeping better these days. I supposed it was necessary, in order to keep up on all of her obligations.

On my last trip outside to load up the fridge, Hunch attempted to follow me out the door of the house.

"We'll be cooking in someone else's house all afternoon and evening, Hunch. You don't want to be stuck outside in the cold van and I can't let you inside."

Whether or not he understood me, I couldn't tell, as he simply headed onto the front porch and sniffed around at the edge of the snow, like he wasn't willing to admit he'd ever wanted to actually come along.

Within ten minutes, Tabby was in the passenger seat and we headed across Honeysuckle Grove and up the mountain toward the Peterson's mansion.

"Sometimes our wealthier clients prefer us to cook in the van, but with the weather, I asked if we could use their kitchen," I explained.

"They would really make you cook outside?" Tabby asked.

"You'd be surprised at some of the things we've been asked to do. Once we had to babysit the owner's children while we cooked, or there was one time we were given a very specific and very strange menu to prepare." Because I didn't particularly want to spend time remembering they clam chowder ice pops that had almost done in my stomach, I said, "But Amber knows the daughter from high school, so I don't imagine they'll push too many odd requests on us."

"Sure, but they're not friends, right?" Tabby pointed out, recalling what Amber had said a couple of days ago.

I sighed. "As long as they weren't enemies, hopefully we can work it in our favor." Amber hadn't had a lot of close friends in high school, but if anybody had befriended her, I would have expected it to be someone else from a wealthy family in town. Amber had grown up in one of the mansions up the mountain, and while her family wasn't as well-to-do as they once were since her father's death, there was a definite class distinction in Honeysuckle Grove.

The Peterson's mansion came into view, standing picturesque against the backdrop of white snow. Soft twinkling lights lined each eave and window frame, and a garland, of pine branches and clusters of crimson berries wound its way along the mansion's ornate wrought-iron fence. On the large wide porch, a life-sized wooden nutcracker stood guard.

"Wow!" Tabby said, breathily.

I'd seen enough West Virginia mansions that I wasn't as easily impressed, but I still loved any home decorated well for Christmas. I pulled into the Peterson's roundabout driveway and looked for a side entrance. It was difficult to see, as the side entrance had not been plowed.

"That's where I was told to bring our supplies in," I said, pointing to a side door, "but I think this is the closest I'm going to be able to park the van without getting stuck."

Tabby looked down at her ankle-high boots, which were soon to be filled with snow. But then her voice came back as chipper as it had ever been. "Alright. Do you want to go talk to the client, while I get everything loaded near the door in the back?" She motioned to the back compartment of the van.

I nodded. "Sounds good. If Amber shows up before I get back, she can help you."

I left Tabby, glad to have worn my knee-high winter boots as I stomped through the snow. I kicked snow out of the way as best as I could to try to clear a path for us to bring our food in. It was hard not to be annoyed at the oversight—the woman had told me to only use the side entrance. The least she could have done was had it cleared for us.

I knocked on the side door three times, and when there was still no answer, I huffed out a breath and then waded back through the snow toward the front entrance. It was elaborate with low sweeping cement steps and two lion-shaped statues on either side of the double front doors. Every inch of this entrance had been cleared of snow.

I stepped up beside the nutcracker and rang the doorbell. A moment later a tall man swung the door open.

"Yes, may I help you?" The fifty-something man looked over a pair of rectangular glasses at me. I wrenched my neck to look up at him. He must have been almost seven feet tall, and thin as a rail.

"Hi! I'm Mallory Beck, the caterer for tonight?" I asked it as a question, because I wasn't entirely sure if this man was a butler or housekeeper, or perhaps the man of the house. "May I speak with Mrs. Peterson?" I asked, when he still hadn't replied and I was starting to shiver.

"Just a moment, please." And then he shut the door in my face.

Thankfully, I barely had time to register my shock before the door swung open again. The woman on the other side wore a tight green sweater with a matching pencil skirt and bare feet, which made me think her floor had to be heated. I shivered again.

"I thought I told you to use the side entrance," she said in way of a greeting. I'd only spoken to the woman on the phone, and I didn't appreciate the scowl she was giving me.

"Well, yes, and I trudged through the snow and knocked three times, but it seems that nobody heard me." Now I was really getting annoyed. I had taken this booking as a favor, as I'd thought at the time that Amber had been friends with the daughter. I could have been enjoying Tabby's company with hot chocolates in hand back in my warm home.

Mrs. Peterson rolled her eyes and called, "Benedict? Did you forget to open the side entrance like I asked?"

The seven-foot man reappeared. "I'll do it now." His voice came out in a slow drawl, not seeming very apologetic for the oversight.

The woman faced me again. "Good enough?" She didn't wait for my answer and shut the door.

My whole snowy trek back to the van, I shook my head. Why had I thought it would be a good idea to bring Tabby to this event? Sure, she could make specialty coffees for the attendees, but what if all of them were as thankless as the woman of the house?

I reached for the door, and as I opened it, I started to say, "I'm sorry. I probably shouldn't have brought you along—"

But she turned from where she'd been squatting near the far end of the van and interrupted me. "Mallory, I think we have a problem."

And that's when I could see past her to my cat, who had apparently stowed away.

Chapter Five - Tabby

MALLORY TRIED TO KEEP a smile on her face, but I could sense she was losing her humor fast over the situation. We couldn't very well leave the cat in the van all evening. Poor little Hunch would freeze to death.

"Do we have time to drive him back?" I asked.

Mallory shook her head. "We might have had time, if the side driveway had been cleared and they were ready for us." She sighed. "Let's get unpacked and then I'll figure something out."

I followed her through the snow and into a side mudroom. An ultra-tall man in black dress pants and a white short-sleeve polo shirt watched us as we brought load after load of food and supplies into the nearby kitchen, but he didn't lift a finger to help us.

On one of our final trips back to the van, I kept my voice quiet as I suggested, "I wonder if they would let you keep Hunch in the mudroom while we work."

Mallory nibbled her lip, passing me a bin of items from the catering van's refrigerator. "I was hoping Amber would be here by now, and maybe she would have time to drive him back to my place."

I knew I should probably offer to help with this, as I wouldn't be needed to prep food for the next couple of hours, but I wasn't super comfortable driving in snow—especially in this amount of snow. Nor would I be comfortable driving this big catering van.

Still, I had to help.

But just as I opened my mouth to offer, Mallory swept Hunch up into her arms and said, "Amber would tell me it's easier to ask forgiveness than permission."

Inside the small mudroom, I nudged the door into the kitchen closed while Mallory placed Hunch under a raised shelf filled with boots. In the sternest voice I'd heard out of her, she whispered, "Now you stay here and out of sight or I'm going to get fired."

While I didn't believe for a second that Hunch would remain under the shelf all day, I somehow knew that the cat was smart like Sherlock. He knew enough to remain invisible.

The mudroom was just as tastefully decorated as the exterior of the mansion, with white coat racks and cubbies along an entire wall, framed by a pine garland. There was a plush armchair in the corner, I supposed only for the purpose of putting on and taking off footwear. A red and green silk swatch draped the back of it, to bring some holiday spirit even to this room. I slid out of my boots and was surprised by the warmth of the floor. Heated floors? These folks must be rich.

The kitchen we had moved our supplies to was actually quite a mess, and so I opened the dishwasher and loaded dirty dishes into it while Mallory texted Amber, instructing her to use the side entrance and to make sure not to let on that Hunch was in the mudroom. I recalled what Mallory had told me about some of the parties she'd catered, where they'd expected her to babysit their children, all while cooking and serving their delicacies. I supposed leaving a messy kitchen for us was at least better than that, but I had to admit, in such a large mansion, I was surprised they didn't have a cook or a housekeeper who would have taken care of this.

The tall thin man continued to wander in and out of the kitchen, not for anything in particular, and so I had to guess he was only here to keep an eye on us. He kept silent, and even as Mallory unloaded her supplies onto the now-clean island, neither of them spoke a word to each other.

It was eerily quiet, and because Mallory wasn't saying anything, I didn't either. Were we going to work in silence all day? I helped unload the supplies, taking note of the few Christmas accessories in the kitchen—a set of old-fashioned Santa tea towels and a row of snowmen canisters along the back of the counter.

I was just getting used to the quiet when Amber burst through the mudroom door, a flurry of energetic noise—or at least it seemed that way in the silent house.

"I'm so sorry! I can't believe I slept through my alarm. There was so much to do at the police station last night and my mind wouldn't shut down when I got home. Then my mind wouldn't shut down because I started thinking about our menu and I hoped you hadn't forgotten to get the capers."

Mallory held up a jar, her countenance instantly brightening with Amber's arrival. "Got 'em."

"Oh, thank goodness." Amber wore a purple short-sleeve sweater with black pants. Every other time I'd seen her, she'd been in a hoodie with some sort of bold saying on the front. I had the impression this was as dressed up as she got. "Did you thaw the puff pastry? Did you bring the crepe maker?" At Mallory's nods, she turned to me. "Oh, hi, Tabby! Are you going to make coffees?"

"That's what I'm here for," I said, hoisting my coffee supplies up onto an empty chunk of counter. The owners of the mansion also had an espresso maker, but theirs was old, and I had no idea if we were allowed to use it, so I got busy setting up the one I'd given to

Mallory and Amber. Apparently Amber had freaked out, via text, when Mallory had told her about my gift. "Can I make something for either of you to enjoy while you work?"

I hadn't even finished my question when Amber chirped, "Peppermint mocha, please!"

I chuckled and dug for the mint syrup from my supplies.

Mallory's and Amber's specialty coffees quickly got cold as they sunk themselves into their work and forgot about them after a sip or two. I had planned to make them fresh ones, but then Amber said to me, "Mallory says you're already an expert on the slicer. You want to finish these peppers while I go check on Hunch?"

While I loved cats, I definitely thought she was the better person to check on that particular cat, so I got to work, glad that I could contribute. As I helped with slicing and dicing, I kept one eye on Mallory and then Amber when she returned. They were both so proficient in the kitchen, and while I didn't know what they were making, it was enjoyable to watch them fill triangles of puff pastry with cream cheese and cranberries, or butterfly the pork tenderloin and fill it with herbs and capers.

"My mouth is watering, and most of it isn't even cooked yet," I told them.

"Well, we'd better get it in the oven soon," Amber told me, "or we'll be serving salmonella."

Mallory shushed Amber from using that word too loudly, and just in time, too, because right then the lady of the house entered the kitchen. She held her cell phone in one hand, typing with her thumb, while carrying a pair of strappy high heels in the other.

"People will be arriving at any minute. I hope you have some appetizers ready." Mrs. Peterson looked at me as she said this, as if I was the chef here. I turned to Mallory, but she was already answering.

"All ready to go in the fridge, and the hot hors d'oeuvres are in the warming tray. Would you like to try one?" Mallory lifted the lid to reveal four varieties of warmed appetizers—miniature quiche and boneless wings and parmesan zucchini spears, and shrimp in phyllo cups.

The woman looked back at her phone. "Oh, I couldn't possibly."

I wondered if it happened often that a woman would hire caterers and then not eat anything they cooked. While she wasn't nearly as thin as the man who had been hovering all day, she did look fit.

"Now shall I have Rhonda prepare the cocktail table in the sitting room for the appetizers or will you be bringing them around?"

By her tone, it was clear she expected the latter, and yet, I could tell by Amber and Mallory's quick look to one another that they really didn't have time to walk around with trays of food if they were expected to have the main meal ready on time.

"I can bring some around," I volunteered, not having any idea what a cocktail table was.

"But we should also probably have some room on the cocktail table as well," Mallory quickly put in. "For the cold appetizers."

"Very well, then," Mrs. Peterson said. It seemed there wasn't any making this woman smile. Then again, if she never ate, it made sense why she was so unhappy.

A man swept into the room. He had curly brown hair with snowflakes still in it, and wore a button-down shirt with the top two buttons open. "Mmm, smells good," he said, heading straight for the warming tray and popping a shrimp cup into his mouth. "The food on my flight was completely inedible."

"Conrad!" Mrs. Peterson admonished. "Save those for the guests."

Conrad was my dad's name, and not a very common one. No one ever spoke in that tone to my father, so it caught me off guard for a second.

"Oh, come on, Emily. They can make more. Can't you ladies?" Conrad gave us all a fleeting look. He was the kind of wealthy man who expected nothing would be a hassle if he threw enough money at it. That was clear in the way he held himself, while his wife, Emily, seemed to be stressing over every last detail.

"Victoria, you must be cooking up something good for tonight," came another male voice from outside the room. This voice was older, and so it didn't surprise me when a cane entered the kitchen before the stooped white-haired man did. "What's this?"

he asked, holding his free hand out toward the three of us behind the island. "Where's Victoria?"

"I gave her the night off," Emily Peterson said, again looking at her phone, but now angling slightly away from the old man. "Poor lady has been working so hard, so I thought she needed a break."

"A break? On the night of our famed Christmas party?" The old man let out something between a laugh and a shriek. "You have got to be kidding me!" He gave a look to Conrad, shook his head, and said, "See? I've been warning you about this kind of overstepping, Son."

The old man turned back toward the door to the rest of the house, waved a backhand toward all of us, and said, "Well, then, I'm not going to bother with it. I'll spend the night in the tub." His voice became a grumble. "It's where I really want to be, anyway."

As soon as he was out of the room, Conrad hissed toward Emily, "You didn't think to run it by him before bringing in someone new to cook for the night?"

As Emily turned and headed for the door, her words to him trailed behind her. "It's not like I fired her, which is what I should have done. I gave her one night off. He'll get over it!"

Conrad followed Emily out of the room, and their voices faded with them.

"Wow!" I whispered to Mallory and Amber. "Do you feel as unwanted as I do?"

Amber, unsurprisingly, came back at normal volume. "It wouldn't be the first time there was fighting over hiring us. Usually it comes down to the money, though."

Mallory shushed her young friend, to which Amber only rolled her eyes.

"I think that old guy must be Cindra's grandfather. She always said he held the purse strings for the family. Conrad's her dad, and the ice queen there is his second wife—Cindra couldn't stand her in high school when she first got together with her dad. Can't say I blame her."

"Who's the tall guy?" I asked, enamored by all the information Amber seemed to have about this family.

But she only shrugged and said, "No idea."

Mallory looked uncomfortable about us discussing their clients and brought the conversation back to a generalization. "It's not unusual to be privy to family arguments when you're in a family's home during the stressful lead-up to a party." Then she dropped her voice just above a whisper. "Mr. and Mrs. Peterson will work things out between them, and she's the one who hired me, so let's just put on the best spread we can, and hopefully that will make it a nonissue."

Mallory and Amber went to set out trays of cold appetizers onto the cocktail table in the living room, but before they left, Mallory called back to me, "I think I left my salt and pepper in the van." I turned for the mudroom, but Mallory interrupted my trek with, "Just check the cupboards. I'm sure they have some."

I had to admit, it felt invasive, going through someone else's cupboards. But I was going to have to work up the nerve to walk around with some of the warm appetizers while Mallory and Amber kept working on cooking the dinner and look like I was comfortable doing it, so I squared my shoulders and opened the upper cupboards one by one.

Unfortunately, if I was busy serving, it wouldn't allow me to make specialty coffee for folks, but I figured those might work better with dessert anyway, and Mallory and Amber would be done cooking by then.

I stopped and blinked a few times at the fourth cupboard I'd opened. It had a whole row of individual spice grinders exactly like the one we had found under Mallory's Christmas tree—except most of these ones were double the size. I pulled one out to study it and was surprised to see there was another row of them behind.

Several of these ones had labels, and I soon found that the largest ones on the right-hand side were filled with salt and pepper. I set those both out on the island, unsure if Mallory wanted them for seasoning as she cooked, or if she planned to have them on the table. While I had the cupboard open, I pulled the others out one by one. Could Amber have come here ahead of time to plant our next clue?

When I didn't find anything, I started to fill an empty tray with a variety of warmed appetizers at the sound of the doorbell.

"How many people are we expecting?" Amber asked as they re-entered the kitchen.

"Twenty-two," Mallory told her. "Which reminds me... I asked that Mrs. Peterson have the dining room table set for dinner ahead of time, but do you want to double check?"

"On it." Amber wiped her hands on her apron and headed out of the room.

Twenty-two guests didn't seem too overwhelming, although I was eager to see a dining room table that would seat so many.

The doorbell rang again and I picked up my tray. Mallory would see the grinders when she got back to cooking, and I'd talk to her about the similarity later, when we had more time. "I'll go and make the rounds with the first few guests."

"Thanks, Tabby," Mallory said. "Are you sure you don't mind?"

"Happy I can help." I headed through the door, just as the doorbell rang again. A twenty-something woman in black dress pants and a blouse, covered by a white apron, headed to answer the door. Her ebony hair was just long enough to be fastened behind her neck in a tight bun.

The living room was massive and filled with holiday cheer. A towering Christmas tree stood near the floor-to-ceiling windows, and reached up toward the high ceiling. Its branches were decorated with an assortment of expensive-looking glass baubles in shades of deep burgundy and emerald. An assortment of gold and silver wrapped gifts lay under the tree, and I had to wonder if they were only empty boxes, or if this family had not opened their presents yet.

Or perhaps that would be part of the festivities tonight.

Plush armchairs and sofas were covered in tasteful holiday-colored accent pillows, but none of the few guests who had arrived were sitting. Christmas music played softly in the background, and I decided I liked the idea of having a Christmas party after the holiday. It made it feel like you could stretch out the celebration to a time that was less frantic.

I brought the tray of warm appetizers toward the two couples who were already in the living room and had found each other. At the last second, I realized

I'd forgotten napkins, so I sidestepped toward the cocktail table—which really just looked like a low coffee table, draped in a gold tablecloth—to grab a few that Mallory or Amber had laid out.

As I approached the two couples, one of the men was saying, "I heard he's not even coming down for his own party. Decided hanging out in his hot tub would be more fun." The man had reddish curly hair and a jovial voice that made everything sound humorous. "I say it's only an avoidance tactic."

"To be fair, Pete, Melvin is in a lot of pain," the woman beside him said. She was gorgeous with platinum blonde hair and meticulously applied makeup. She was almost as tall as Pete, the redheaded man, and he was by no means short.

I cleared my throat, so as not to seem like I was eavesdropping, even if I was, and said, "May I offer you a warm appetizer?"

"Oooh, something warm sounds so nice." As the blonde helped herself to a zucchini wedge, I was tempted to suggest she remove her shoes if she wanted to warm up, but I was afraid she might find it rude rather than humorous.

The other couple helped themselves to a warm shrimp cup each and continued speaking as if I weren't there.

"Melvin wouldn't even have the option of the hot tub if I hadn't fixed it for him this week," the stockier man who looked uncomfortable in his navy suit said. He had a long beard and a disgruntled expression as he added, "I'll bet it's the only reason we were even invited."

"Oh come on, Jerry," the woman beside him said, pulling herself close to his arm. "They invite us every year."

"Yeah, at the last minute," Jerry grumbled.

While I wanted to hear more, I knew pausing for another ten seconds would appear conspicuous. I'd eavesdropped on enough conversations at The Heirloom Café back in Crystal Cove to know how long I could remain invisible.

Speaking of invisible, after taking only two steps away from the grouping, I stilled as two cat eyes blinked at me from underneath the couch at the far wall. Hunch! Mallory would not be pleased. But at the same time, I couldn't very well pull him out of there without anyone noticing. Mallory and Amber were far too busy to worry about this right now.

I wondered if I could somehow distract the four guests and send them to another room for just long enough for me to retrieve the cat.

But that thought was barely through my head when suddenly there were six guests, and then eight, and then twelve.

I pasted on a smile and served each one of them, praying that none of them would spend any time looking under the furniture.

Chapter Six - Mallory

"THE TABLE ISN'T SET or even cleared," Amber said with a huff as she marched back into the kitchen. She was going to get us fired with her loud complaining voice, but at the same time, I was irritated enough that I almost didn't care.

"Alright, well, you know the drill."

She sighed a laborious sigh. "Yeah, I'll do it. But can you make sure the tenderloin doesn't overcook?"

"You bet," I told her.

She ducked into the mudroom, I assumed to check on Hunch, first. She was back a second later and headed for the dining room, not saying another word to me. I was glad she wasn't going on about the disrespect of our clients, which she had done more than once in the past.

As much as I loved having Amber around, I also appreciated having a kitchen to myself here and there for a few minutes. As soon as she was out of the room, I started humming as I worked at mashing the garlicky potatoes. In an instant, the stress of the day fell off me. We were good at this, Amber and I, and soon the whole dinner party would know it.

Before I had much time to relax, Mr. and Mrs. Peterson pushed through the door into the kitchen, in mid-whispered argument.

"Everyone has noticed and it's all they're going to be talking about," Mrs. Peterson hissed.

Mr. Peterson sighed. "There's nothing about it we can do about it when he's made up his mind. You know that."

"Well there's something I can do!" Without even taking notice of me, Mrs. Peterson spun and marched back through the door, with her husband on her heels. I was just glad they didn't seem to be upset over our food or the fact that we were the ones preparing it.

I had only just finished transferring the mashed potatoes to a serving dish, when Tabby returned to the kitchen with an empty tray.

"They love your appetizers. Are you able to make more shrimp cups, or is this the last of them?"

I smiled, always happy to hear when one of Amber's creations was a hit. "That's the end of them, but let the guests know that we'll have them seated for the main course in about five minutes." With a rolling hand motion, I encouraged her to refill her tray with the remaining appetizers from the warmer. "That should tide them over." As she carefully arranged the appetizers on her tray, I added, "How are everyone's spirits? Are they enjoying the party?"

With her full tray, she leaned closer and whispered, "To be honest, I think they're all a little perturbed that Melvin didn't show up for his own party. I'm pretty sure it's that old man who was in here earlier. I can kind of understand why he didn't—no one seems to have a nice thing to say about the man—but finally Mrs. Peterson headed upstairs, saying she'd do her best to get him to join them at least for dinner." That must have been what Mr. and Mrs. Peterson had been arguing about. I was curious to see if she would be able to convince the old crotchety man about anything. Tabby checked over her shoulder before adding, "I personally think the dinner would be more enjoyable without the man, but it's not my party."

I grinned at her phrasing, as it was the same phrasing I'd been trying to teach Amber to use regarding our catering events for months. It's not our party.

Tabby turned to head out with her replenished tray of appetizers, but

before she could take her second
step toward the kitchen door, a
blood-curdling scream echoed from
somewhere on the other side of it.

Chapter Seven – Tabby

I FROZE IN PLACE, the tray almost toppling to the floor. "What was that?"

It wasn't a true question, because I realized Mallory didn't know the answer any better than I did. I raced through the kitchen door toward the living room, placing my tray down on the nearest hutch as I went.

There had to be twenty people here now, and I looked around at every face that I'd encountered at least once tonight to see who had screamed, but all eyes were on the extra-wide stairway that led to the upper floor. The ultra-tall and thin man now wore a baby blue dress shirt and stood over by the couch that Hunch had once been underneath, but I could no longer see that cat anywhere.

"Is everyone okay?" I asked in my loudest and most commanding tone—which admittedly was not terribly loud nor commanding. No one answered me, and I looked around for the owners of the house, the Petersons. They had come back into the living room only a few moments before me, but now were missing.

Had they gone upstairs? Had it been his wife who had screamed from up there? The scream had been so loud, it surprised me it could have come from all the way on the upper floor.

Amber appeared through the dining room door, and Mallory, who had followed me in from the kitchen said to her, "Amber, take care of the kitchen for a minute. I'm going to go see what happened."

Amber nodded and a second later retreated to the kitchen. I was torn between following Mallory or following Amber, or somehow trying to calm the people who had now worked themselves into a frenzied chatter in the living room. I paused for a second, and when it seemed like gossip would keep people in one place for the moment, I bounded up the stairs after Mallory. I was too curious not to.

"It's an old hot tub, dear." Conrad Peterson was rubbing his wife's back as I found them in an upstairs hallway. She seemed inconsolable. "I told him it was bound to happen."

"It's your dad!" She sobbed into his chest. "Don't you even care that he's dead?"

My eyes widened. Had Melvin died in the hot tub right in the middle of the dinner party? And was Conrad indicating that it had happened due to a hot tub malfunction, and not simply due to old age or the many, many ailments I'd overheard the man suffered from?

"Oh, you know Dad," Conrad said, and he truly did sound too casual for someone who had only just lost his father. "He always told us he'd rather go in an instant than suffer through years of pain."

"He was joking," Emily Peterson said. In contrast to her blasé husband, her voice shook as she asked, "Was the tub too hot for him? There were burns on his back."

Conrad shook his head. "I had Jerry turn it down to ninety when he was in doing maintenance on it earlier this week."

"Jerry?" Emily's forehead buckled like this concerned her. She looked in the direction of the stairs and then nodded as she said, "Jerry was here working on it," as though she'd just remembered the same thing herself.

"Did you move him at all?" Mallory asked in a gentle voice, emerging from a room just down the hall. "Or was he like that when you found him?"

Mr. Peterson's face morphed into a scowl. "Of course we didn't move him! We only found him like that a moment ago."

Mallory nodded, seemingly unfazed by the man's tone, and pulled out her phone to start texting. I assumed she was getting in touch with Alex and I was impressed at her ability to stay cool in a stressful situation. "I'll get in touch with the paramedics and the police will be here soon. They will want—"

"The police!" Mrs. Peterson exclaimed. "Why on earth would you call the police?"

Mallory held up her hands like she was under arrest. "I'm afraid a sudden death of any kind has to be reported." The woman looked to her husband and something unspoken passed between them. "Now, I'm just going to ensure that the hot tub is turned off and that everything stays put until the police arrive." Her voice didn't leave any room for argument, and when she marched back into the room she'd come out of. I was left to face off with the couple.

I had no idea what to say as their gazes both bore into mine. Finally, I came up with, "I think your guests would appreciate an update."

The couple looked to each other again and then swiftly headed for the stairs. The moment they were out of my eye line, I moved ahead to the doorway Mallory had ducked through.

"Mallory?" I called her name, since she was distracted, leaning over the old man in the hot tub.

"I'm not sure you want to come in here," she told me. "Just direct Alex upstairs when he gets here. Apparently, the town paramedics are all at a bus accident, but I'm certain it's too late for this man, anyway."

I moved into the room, regardless of her instructions. I couldn't leave her in here alone, and besides, it actually wouldn't be the first time I'd seen a dead body in a tub—although the last time, it had been full of dry ice.

I stopped just inside the double doors that were now wide open to what looked like a solarium, with windows around three sides and a glass roof. Right in the center of the dimly lit room was a large hot tub. I wondered if there was concern over the weight of the hot tub up here on the second floor, or if they had specifically designed the house with it in mind. I had to guess from the look of the solarium that it had been built specifically for it.

It was a habit of mine, while around a dead body, to focus on my other surroundings. I took in the free-standing towel cabinet, which looked much fancier than the ones we had checked out at the hardware store this morning, and the two brass free-standing towel racks, both decorated in a nautical theme. When I finally forced myself to look back to Mallory, she had a hand on the old man's neck. He was slumped forward with his face almost in the water. The jets and the lighting had been turned off, so everything inside the tub seemed very dark and still.

"There's definitely no pulse," she said, pulling her hand away. "I don't want to move him before Alex gets here, but at the same time, I'm afraid the weight of his head might pull him forward into the water."

I looked back at the towel racks. When I set my eyes on a decorative life preserver with the words "Peterson's Tub" inscribed on it, I walked toward it. "I wonder if this actually floats." I pulled it away from the rack and passed it to Mallory.

She set it under the man's head, immediately catching onto my suggestion, but until he actually fell onto it, it wouldn't hold him in place. I reached over and grabbed some decorative rope from another towel rack and Mallory helped me as we secured the life preserver to metal hooks on either side of the tub.

"That way he won't go under and it'll be easier for the medical examiner to determine what happened to him."

I nodded to Mallory's explanation, even though I didn't need one. It was the exact thing Jay had taught me regarding the scene of any death—do what you can to preserve the body as you find it.

Once we were done securing the preserver, Mallory grabbed for another nearby rope and said, "Come on. I'm sure the Peterson's have gotten rid of most of their guests by now, but there are always a few straggling lookie-loos who are too curious for their own good. Let's rope off the bottom of the stairs."

I followed her lead, but by the time we arrived at the bottom of the stairs, we heard chatter from the dining room. Lots of chatter.

"You don't think...?" I started, at the same time Mallory said, "Are they going ahead with the dinner?"

The words were no sooner out of her mouth when Amber pushed through from the kitchen, holding a giant tray with individual salads.

"They all stayed?" Mallory asked.

"I suggested the food was ready anyway. I had no idea what was going on upstairs, but I figured if anyone needed to be questioned..."

"You're always one step ahead," Mallory said with a relieved smile. "That makes more sense. I thought the Petersons were the ones pushing to keep the meal on track."

"Oh, they were. But then it seemed like a good idea, so I encouraged it. What happened?" She motioned with her head to the upper floor.

"A death, unfortunately." Mallory shook her head. "Looks like just a malfunction of an old hot tub. Alex is on his way."

Amber nodded, shifting her weight. I could tell her arms were getting tired from holding the large tray, so I swept in and took it from her. She didn't fight me on it, and while Mallory explained the details to Amber, I headed for the dining room to drop off the salads and at least keep the crowd happy.

I hadn't been wrong about the dining room table. It was impressive—long enough to accommodate all twenty-two guests, although two place settings sat empty. I assumed the one at the head of the table had been intended for the recently deceased, so I guessed there had either been one no-show, or one person who had been frightened off by Mrs. Peterson's scream.

The chatter stopped as soon as I entered the room and everyone looked at me. They all seemed cheery enough, so I wondered what Mr. and Mrs. Peterson had told them. I pasted on a smile. "I think you'll enjoy this first course salad," I said brightly, looking down at the salads for the first time. They were beautifully plated, and as I started to set them in front of each guest, I took in the brightly colored thin-sliced radish, laid among some sort of shredded cheese on a bed of kale. I, of course, had no idea what it would taste like, and what kind of dressing Mallory and Amber had chosen, so I just placed each plate down to let the flavors speak for themselves.

When I arrived near the empty seat at the head of the table where Mr. and Mrs. Peterson sat, Mr. Peterson murmured to me, "Let me know when the police arrive, will you?" His low voice and pasted-on smile made me wonder if they were trying to pretend to their guests that nothing at all was out of the ordinary.

The tall thin man sat beside Mrs. Peterson and the two of them were whispering to one another with similar pasted-on smiles. If the tall man was sitting down to dinner, he clearly wasn't staff. I wondered if he was family or just a close enough friend that he would have been welcome well before the start of the party.

As I arrived back in the living room, Mallory was still updating Amber on the situation, and had her phone in her hands, her thumbs flying over it. I guessed she was updating Alex.

"So if there's no foul play, should we encourage them to leave?" Amber asked.

"Not just yet. Let's see what Alex says when he gets here. You did the right thing, keeping everyone, and besides, it would be a shame for all our food to go to waste."

"I think they're pretending to their guests that nothing important happened," I told them.

As Mallory turned to me with a raised eyebrow, a flash of movement caught my eye from the top of the stairs. When I looked up, there was no one. I'd have thought it was Hunch, but what I'd seen was definitely larger than a cat.

"Could anyone have gone up there?" I asked, just to make sure.

Mallory shook her head. "We've been right here the whole time."

I thought of the empty place setting and wondered if someone could have gone up there prior to dinner—prior to Mrs. Peterson finding her father-in-law in the bathtub—perhaps to find a bathroom or something.

Mrs. Peterson had followed me from the dining room, making me jump when her voice sounded from behind me. "I would appreciate you ladies keeping the food coming, not leaving too much dead space where folks are going to start speculating about what happened." Her gaze landed on the rope at the bottom of the stairway. "Oh no. Let's get that out of here!"

Mallory placed a hand on her arm. "We have to leave it at least until the police arrive."

"That's another thing. Why you thought you had to call the police, I'll never know." Before Mallory could argue with her about protocol, she went on. "I trust you will somehow keep that quiet as well." Thankfully, she stepped back from the rope.

As Mallory nodded, I had to ask. "Could someone still be upstairs?"

I was talking about the empty place setting, but Mrs. Peterson misunderstood. "Oh, Victoria? No, whenever I give our regular chef the night off, she stays at her boyfriend's house across town."

I thought again about how disappointed Melvin had been that Victoria hadn't been here cooking for the dinner party tonight. I wondered if this Victoria lady would be equally disappointed that she hadn't gotten to see Melvin one more time before he died.

"So the extra place setting at the table...?" I asked, still wondering who hadn't made it here, and if a late arrival might interfere with us keeping the police's arrival as quiet as possible.

"That's mine," a voice said from the top of the stairs. We all looked up to see a teenage girl. "I know, I'm late. Couldn't be helped." She didn't sound apologetic in the least in her monotone. She wore low-riding dirty jeans and a black Harley Davidson t-shirt. The sleeves had been cut off to reveal very muscular arms, especially for a teenage girl.

"You are not wearing that to dinner, Cindra!" Mrs. Peterson hissed.

Cindra. Wasn't that the girl Amber knew from high school. She'd said Cindra was a snob, but this girl didn't really look like a snob.

The girl let out a laborious sigh. "Well, I'm starving. If I have to shower and change, I might as well skip dinner, anyway." Her gaze set on Amber. "Oh. Hey, Amber."

Amber held up a hand for a silent wave, clearly not wanting to get in the middle of the mother/daughter argument.

"You promised," her mother hissed, and then spun and headed back for the dining room.

Cindra watched her go and then turned back toward us. "You guys are catering, right? Are you going to starve me, too, or can I grab something before she comes back?"

I had to suck in my lips to keep from smiling at this girl's attitude. Maybe she'd been a snob at school, but at home it seemed she was the farthest thing from slipping into her parents' snobby mold.

"Come on," Amber said, surprising me. "I'll grab you a plate."

As soon as they were out of the room, I asked Mallory, "Do you think it's okay that Cindra's upstairs?" I looked to the rope that she had easily stepped over and not even asked about. "Should we at least tell her about her grandfather?"

Mallory nodded. "You're probably right. The upstairs is huge, and there's a good chance her room is nowhere near the hot tub, but if her parents aren't going to mention it, we probably should." Mallory sighed, and I felt her pain. It was never pleasant, having to deliver the news of the deceased. Although, I had a feeling this Cindra girl would take it in stride.

A moment later, Cindra led the way back through the kitchen door with a heaping plate of tenderloin and garlic mashed potatoes and julienned buttered vegetables. "This looks really good. Thanks, guys."

She was headed for the stairs, but Mallory stopped her. "Cindra, can I get you to just sit here and eat in the living room for a minute? I have something I have to talk to you about."

She raised an eyebrow. I looked down at her hands, holding her plate, and her fingernails were blunt and rimmed with dirt or grease.

She didn't sit, but she at least faced Mallory, her feet wide, like she was in some kind of a power stance. "What is it?"

"We didn't realize anyone else was upstairs," Mallory started, glancing at the plush couch again, but she didn't make a move toward it.

I recalled the flash of movement I'd seen at the top of the stairs, and I had to wonder if her attitude was to cover her truly being shaken up over seeing something upsetting.

"Have you gone near the hot tub recently?" I blurted, interrupting whatever Mallory was about to say.

Again with the raised eyebrow. "No. No one uses it except Gramps."

Uh-oh. The nickname suggested they were close. Thankfully, Mallory took over.

"Your grandfather...well, there was an unfortunate accident tonight, Cindra." Mallory reached over to stroke Cindra's arm, but she pulled her hand away just as fast at Cindra's stiffening over the approaching touch.

"What? He finally died in his own hot tub?" she asked with the slightest smile, like she must have been joking.

But at Mallory's slow nod, Cindra's face drooped. "Are you sure? Did it happen suddenly?"

"We think so," Mallory told her. "It looked like the hot tub may have malfunctioned. Apparently it's old, and, well, your mom found him not too long ago."

"Emily is not my mother." Cindra looked like she'd sucked on a lemon.

"Oh." Mallory seemed taken aback. "I'm sorry. I meant Mrs. Peterson." She took in a big breath as if resetting herself. "Look, Cindra, I know hearing something like this isn't easy..."

She shrugged. "Oh, I'm fine. I mean, he was old. He wanted to die and better that he went quickly than suffer through more years of his cluster headaches and arthritis." She really sounded as unbothered by this as her father. "Is he still up there?" She motioned her head toward the upper floor, as her hands were still full with her heaping plate.

Mallory nodded. "We have to leave everything as it is until the police arrive."

"The police?" Cindra pulled back. It was the first bit of surprise I'd really seen on her face.

"Yes. Whenever there's a sudden death, even at home, the police will want to have a look before the person is moved. But you can just avoid that part of the house until they've been in and done their thing."

"You know who's really going to be upset by this is Victoria."

"Victoria... your chef?" Mallory asked.

Cindra nodded. "She loved Gramps, and she was almost the only person he had any patience for. But don't worry. I'll knock on her door and tell her. Thanks for letting me know."

"She had the night off," Mallory explained. "Your Mo—Mrs. Peterson said she would be staying at her boyfriend's place tonight."

Cindra's forehead creased. "Her light was on. I'm pretty sure she's upstairs in her room."

Mallory's nod was slow. "I'll be busy with dinner for the next hour, but I'm happy to talk to her later if you'd rather—"

"Nah, I got it," Cindra said casually. "Is that all you needed to talk to me about?"

A dead grandfather, killed by a malfunctioning hot tub, and awaiting the police? If this teenage girl seemed to think this was nothing to get worked up over, I had to wonder what other kinds of upsets she'd had to endure in her life.

Chapter Eight - Mallory

THE DOORBELL RANG SHORTLY after Cindra had gone upstairs to inform their chef about her grandfather's death. I hoped it was Alex.

"Did Cindra seem as blasé to you as she did to me?" Tabby asked as I headed for the door.

"Yeah, the only thing that ever upset that girl was when someone was better than her at something. She was super competitive in school," Amber was saying as I moved out of earshot. I arrived at the massive front doors at the same time as the housekeeper, Rhonda. I stepped back to let her do her job, but the second I saw it was Alex on the other side, I started talking, giving him the rundown.

"The grandfather of the house, a man probably in his eighties named Melvin, was found without a pulse in the hot tub about twenty minutes ago," I told him.

Rhonda shushed me. "Mr. and Mrs. Peterson asked that you keep this quiet. Can you please have this discussion upstairs?"

Alex pulled off his boots and said to me, "Show me the way."

When we moved through the living room, Tabby was on her own.

"Tabby, this is Alex. Alex, Tabby." I motioned between them.

Alex reached to shake her hand. "I'm sorry we're not meeting under better circumstances."

Tabby gave a conciliatory nod and then turned to me. "Amber went to serve the main course." I was so glad that girl was on top of things, because I had completely forgotten the dinner. "I'll go help her."

I looked between the stairs and the kitchen door and then nodded. "She's great at plating food, but she can be a perfectionist, and if she doesn't have help, the food will be cold by the time she serves it."

"On it!" Tabby told me, heading for the kitchen.

I turned and led the way up the stairs, talking to Alex quietly as I went. "Like I said, Mrs. Peterson found the man. He appears to have burns on his back."

Alex nodded and typed something into his phone. "Right. I'll see if Bob can stop over as soon as he leaves the bus accident." Bob Shone was the town's medical examiner. "So the tub malfunctioned?"

"That's what Mr. Peterson seemed to think. He said the tub was so old, he wasn't surprised." As we made our way down a hallway in the opposite direction of where Cindra had disappeared, I dropped my voice to a whisper. "Neither Mr. Peterson nor his daughter Cindra, who unknown to all of us was upstairs in her room the whole time, seemed particularly upset about it."

"Cindra... the girl Amber went to high school with?"

I nodded. "That's right. Apparently, they weren't really friends."

Alex nodded. "That's what she's been telling me." Amber and Alex got to spend a lot more time with each other than they did with me these days. Aside from the loneliness I struggled with from time to time, I was glad. Amber needed a father figure in her life, and Alex filled the role well. I was only a tiny bit jealous. "I hear Cindra spent all her time in the trades wing in high school and had absolutely no patience for anyone who tried out a course in mechanics or carpentry 'for fun.'"

"Sounds a little like how Amber is in the kitchen, if you ask me. Although, she's been amazingly inviting with Tabby."

All the humor of the situation left me as we turned into the solarium and something had definitely changed. The decorative life preserver Tabby and I had finagled to the sides of the hot tub had come loose and now floated on the side of the hot tub farthest away from Melvin Peterson. Not only that, but Melvin's face was now fully in the water.

"It couldn't be," I said, under my breath.

"What?" Alex asked, pulling out his phone and immediately taking photos of the situation.

"We had the life preserver secured so it would keep his head out of the water," I told Alex. "We tied it up really well." To be fair, I hadn't checked Tabby's knots on her side, but she seemed so proficient at pretty much everything, I couldn't imagine her doing a poor job. Still, I didn't know for sure.

"So you think someone came and untied it?" Alex asked.

I started to doubt myself. "At least my side. I tied it up really well." I motioned to the side metal hook on the edge of the tub that now sat empty.

"You said his granddaughter, Cindra, was upstairs the whole time?" Alex double checked, pausing his typing into his phone to look at me.

I nodded slowly. "But why would she...?" As I started to speak the words, it came to me. "I mean, she said he was really suffering with his arthritis and cluster headaches. She was concerned with whether or not he had died quickly. She said dying quickly was how he wanted to go..."

When I trailed off, Alex read my mind, filling in the blank for me. "So you think it's possible that she doubted he was truly dead, and came in here to make certain of it?"

The way he put it sounded truly morbid, but I had to admit, that was exactly what I was suspecting.

WE WERE JUST FINISHING serving up dinner, which hopefully would keep the guests occupied for a few minutes, when the doorbell rang again. Amber was at the head of the table, nodding to something Mr. and Mrs. Peterson were quietly murmuring to her. While it wasn't our job to answer the door, I had some concern that if the medical examiner or another detective showed up, that housekeeper may turn them away.

I set down the last two plates, told Jerry and Jenny—a couple who had been here since the beginning and I'd approached often enough that I'd learned their names—to enjoy, and then headed through the living room for the front door.

Sure enough, as I made it into the living room, I could hear the housekeeper telling someone in a stern tone, "We're in the middle of a very special dinner party."

Shaking my head at the lack of perspective in this household, I skirted around the corner as the housekeeper, standing in the door's frame, tried to edge the door shut on a man with windblown white hair wearing a long white coat. This had to be the medical examiner.

"I'll quietly show him upstairs," I blurted, even though I was quite sure this man would not so easily be turned away.

The housekeeper looked between me and the white-smocked man, and finally sighed. "Do it quickly," she told me in a sharp whisper. "And you'd both better keep quiet."

I resisted the urge to shake my head at the woman and instead motioned to the medical examiner to follow me. He did, and neither of us said a word until we were at the top of the stairs.

"Right this way," I whispered, leading the way. We made it to the hallway where we had to turn to the right. We were being so quiet, the sudden sob that came from the other direction stopped us both in place. A second later, a blur of movement streaked passed us.

"He can't be dead! He can't be!" A young woman, perhaps in her early to mid-twenties, raced past us wearing a white flowy nightgown that went just past her knees. She clearly had not had time to wash her face before bed, because her mascara was tear streaked down both cheeks.

"It was the guy's time to go," Cindra said, walking fast after her. She glanced at us as she passed. "Sorry. I tried to keep Victoria in her room. I should have known she would be this upset."

This was the house's chef, Victoria? She seemed awfully young to be working as a family's personal chef.

"Don't let her touch anything!" the medical examiner called after Cindra, as he picked up his pace.

I hurried to keep up, and as I arrived at the solarium, it was difficult to know where to look first. At Mallory and Alex, who were stooped near a wall outlet on the far wall, at Victoria, who was sobbing at the edge of the hot tub, with Cindra trying to pull her away by her arm, or at the medical examiner, who walked a slow circle around the hot tub, surveying the situation.

The old man, Melvin, now had his face fully in the water, and the life preserver floated untied across the hot tub from him. I tilted my head, wondering if Mallory and Alex had untied it for some reason.

Thankfully, Cindra was strong and quickly had Victoria away from the tub and out of the room. "You don't want to look at him like that," the young girl told her chef in a monotone.

"The deceased didn't have his face underwater when we found him," I told the medical examiner, my automatic need to help kicking in even though I wanted to get back to help Amber. "Mallory and I..." I motioned to her, wondering how well she knew this medical examiner. Our medical examiner in Crystal Cove finally knew me by name, but that had taken more than a year. Even if Alex had his reasons for removing the life preserver, I'd worked with police and medical professionals often enough that I knew I had to tell my own truth of what I knew. In the end, it never helped to keep things to ourselves. "...We attempted to keep his face out of the water with that life preserver, but for some reason it didn't stay."

Mallory stood and moved to the edge of the tub. "I can't tell you about both sides, but over here..." she motioned to the metal loop she'd tied her side of the rope to, "...I triple knotted it, to be sure it wouldn't come undone."

"I tied a bowline on my side," I put in. "I tie up boats regularly. Someone would have had to have made a concerted effort to untie it."

Mallory dropped her voice to nearly a whisper, even though Victoria's loud wails and what Cindra must have thought of as reassuring words for her had faded off in the distance by this time. "From what we hear, this man, Melvin Peterson, wanted to die quickly. We suspect that perhaps his granddaughter removed the life preserver, just to make certain he was dead."

The medical examiner let out a low sigh. "It's certainly not going to help my assessment." He stepped further around the hot tub. "Then again, it may not matter. By these blisters and burns on his back, I'll likely be able to discover time and cause of death regardless. And with an autopsy, I will be able to ascertain if water was ingested pre or post mortem."

I was glad that the young girl's impulsive move wouldn't cause this to be dragged out. It was never fun to have to explain to family members why forensics teams had to come in and out of their house repeatedly in the midst of their grief over losing someone.

The medical examiner opened a leather bag he had carried upstairs with him and turned to Alex. "You say you think the tub malfunctioned?"

Alex stood. "That's something we need to talk about, Bob."

Before he could go on, Amber appeared in the doorway. Her eyes lingered on the man in the tub for one long second before she turned to Mallory. "You need to help with dessert, or there's no way it'll be plated by the time they're done eating."

Mallory immediately stood and followed her out the door. "Text me if you need anything, Alex. We'll be right downstairs."

I felt bad that I'd gotten so distracted by the investigation that I'd forgotten about Amber. She should have been the one upstairs, having experience with forensics. Then again, I didn't have enough experience in the kitchen to handle that by myself either. I offered a small wave in Alex's direction. I also wished we could have met for the first time under better circumstances.

Before I turned to leave, movement caught my eye, and I was surprised to see Hunch's tail flick from behind one of the towel racks. I paused, wondering if I should mention the cat to either of the men. If it were Sherlock, I'd leave him to help investigate. Amber had once told me they had a very observant cat, but was that enough reason to leave him at the scene of a death?

I sucked in my lips, ready to leave, but I had to at least mention it. I turned back. "Um, Alex?"

He raised his eyebrows at me. I pointed at the towel rack, and because of his vantage point, he could probably see more of the cat than I could. A slight smile quirked up on one side of his lips.

"He's good. But thanks for letting me know."

For some reason it made me like Alex all the more, that he didn't mind a cat being around in the midst of his serious work. I could tell already how good he was for Mallory.

When I entered the kitchen, Mallory and Amber were in the midst of a flurry of activity. There were a dozen dessert plates laid out on the island, each one with a crepe rolled up across it. Amber was working the crepe maker on the other counter, while Mallory was dressing up the top of each crepe with whipped cream and shaved chocolate.

"What can I do?" I asked.

Before I could answer, Mrs. Peterson swept into the room, her face contorting in anger. "My brother tells me all three of you were upstairs consorting with those detectives!" Clearly, her brother hadn't known enough to inform her that there was only one detective so far, and one medical examiner, and the last thing we were doing was consorting. But I bit my tongue to hold in my response as she went on. "I'm paying you to cater this event. Nothing more. Now I hope you can keep your priorities straight long enough to finish your job, so I don't have to fire you all on the spot."

With that, she swept back out of the room and the three of us looked at each other with widened eyes. We weren't the ones who needed to keep our priorities straight.

Chapter Ten - Mallory

Mrs. Peterson was clearly under a lot of stress; however, she wasn't the only one. As I delivered desserts, I took note of the tense whispering between a redheaded man and the bearded man seated beside him. Mr. and Mrs. Peterson both wore forced smiles, but it was obvious they were fake. I had to make a concerted effort not to glare at the tall thin man when he looked in my direction, as I could now see the resemblance between him and Emily Peterson. He'd gone and tattled to his sister about us being upstairs.

I followed Amber and Tabby back to the kitchen.

"She didn't have to be rude to me in front of everybody," Amber said when the door was barely shut behind us.

"Who? Mrs. Peterson?" I set a tray of dirty dishes down on the only clean part of the counter. "What did she say? I didn't hear anything." Amber could tend to exaggerate. In front of everybody often meant that she'd been embarrassed over one person's quiet comment to another.

She yanked open the dishwasher, and I held out my hands for her to calm down. "Mrs. Peterson told that brother of hers that next time she'd hire only adults. It was clearly meant for me to hear."

She was probably right, and Amber tended to get indignant when people called out her age, but I hoped I could get her to calm down about it tonight. Her making waves with our clients, who were obviously taking their stress out on us, would not do anyone any good.

"Let's just get cleaned up, get the job done, and get out," I told her.

We worked in silence for several minutes, and while Amber started clanking dishes against the dishwasher as she loaded it, her clanking soon became less and less. Meanwhile, I scraped plates into the garbage, and rinsed them, and Tabby packed our food and prep materials back into bins.

"Should I bother offering specialty coffees?" she asked. "Or just bring out the pots of regular and decaf?" She motioned to the two carafes she had brewed while Amber and I had been plating dessert.

"Save those for us," Amber grumbled. "Like Mallory said, let's just get done and get out."

While I didn't like that she was still upset, I couldn't disagree with her. I nodded to Tabby and she made the rounds with the two coffee pots. When she returned only a minute later, both carafes were still full.

"Mrs. Peterson said it was far too late for coffee." Tabby set the carafes back onto their warmers. "I tried to tell her we had decaf, but she waved me off and told me to let them enjoy their dessert in peace."

"Wow. Sorry you had to deal with that," I said. "It's clearly an awful evening for them. Maybe the shock of the situation is just setting in now, and they're wishing they'd sent everyone home an hour ago."

I was trying my best to have compassion, but it was difficult when people were rude to my friends. Tabby continued to pack up items, but stopped when she got to the salt and pepper grinders that belonged with the house. I had noticed the similarity to our Christmas gift earlier, but hadn't had time to look closely at them. I was about to remind her that those weren't mine, when she said, "So weird that they have the exact same type of grinders as we found under our tree, right, Amber?" She wore a forced coy smile as she asked, and I could tell she was trying to cheer Amber up. "In fact, they have a whole cupboard full of them. Then again, I couldn't find a single other clue among them. Do you think I'm missing something?"

Amber had stopped loading dishes on the word "clue." Her forehead creased. "A whole cupboard full of what?"

Tabby opened the cupboard. "Spice grinders. Look at them all. And these things aren't cheap. What I don't understand is how you got in here ahead of time. And if you didn't leave the next clue taped to one of the other grinders, where on earth is it?" I thought briefly about the towel cupboard I'd seen in the upstairs solarium, but that thought vanished when Amber shook her head, her face contorting like she was trying to swallow down a bitter hunk of liver.

"Clue? What are you talking about?" she asked.

I knew her well enough to be able to tell she was serious. "We were sure you must be behind what's turning out to be a very tough treasure hunt, but it wasn't you, was it?"

She shook her head, her forehead still creased. "You found a spice grinder under a tree? Under your Christmas tree?" she asked, catching on fast. She definitely wasn't hiding anything. She knew nothing about this.

"Must have been Alex, then," Tabby said, unbothered. "I guess it won't be on our priority list to ask him about it tonight, though."

While her observation seemed lighthearted enough, something about it troubled me. I was no longer completely convinced that the treasure hunt had been constructed by either Alex or Amber. But if not them, who?

And what if we had been wrong about it being a treasure hunt in the first place? What on earth would that mean?

Before this thought had fully formed, I pulled out my phone and snapped several photos of the spice grinders, all lined up neatly across the inside of the cupboard. Most were larger than the one we found under the tree, but that one had contained remnants of saffron, a very expensive spice that was usually used sparingly, so it made sense it was in a smaller spice grinder. I found two other tiny ones like it. One was labeled as celery seed, which is actually something I would have put in a larger spice grinder, myself, as I used it often. The other was unlabeled, but after opening it and giving it a quick sniff, there was no mistaking anise.

"So strange," I murmured, replacing it in the cupboard and shutting the door.

Tabby continued packing, lost in her own thoughts and probably not catching on to my sudden questions over the strangeness of the gift under my tree. Amber, on the other hand, was studying me. I knew she had plenty of questions, especially seeing the contemplative look on my face, but we would get to those later.

For now, I wanted to pack up, get out, and then text Alex to see if they'd found anything noteworthy upstairs. A blackened spot on the outlet cover had led him to checking that out, and discovering that the ground fault circuit interrupter, which I had never heard of, but apparently was represented by the small red and black buttons in the center of it, had not kicked in to cut the power as it should have. He'd planned to call a friend on the forensics team to discuss it, but I figured that had to have been the cause of the malfunctioning hot tub—which, strangely enough, didn't seem to have much to do with the age of the tub.

I had so many questions—about the investigation, but also about the spice grinder, which was starting to give me the creeps. What were the chances there would be the exact same spice grinders in a house where we happened to be catering and Alex happened to be investigating a death?

And if Alex didn't leave it for me, had someone else been inside my house?

Chapter Eleven - Tabby

WHILE THE THREE OF us headed toward the mudroom to stow all the bins of supplies in the catering van, Mallory asked Amber, "You sure you want to go upstairs?" Several other detectives and forensics officers had arrived by this time, and apparently Amber knew them all well, since she had been interning with the forensics team; however, the Petersons had been getting more and more irritable with each new arrival. Amber was so young, I had a hard time with Mallory throwing her to the wolves, so to speak.

"I have to at least let Alex know we're heading out." Amber quirked a smile on one side of her mouth, like she enjoyed the challenge.

"Just... don't make waves," Mallory told her. "Let's leave here with our catering reputation intact."

As Amber headed for the door back into the main part of the house, I had to bring up one more challenge that could very well ruin their catering reputation.

"Um, Amber?" When she looked back, I told her in barely a murmur, "You should probably grab Hunch, too."

Mallory immediately started looking around the lower half of the mudroom. With everything that had gone on tonight, she had clearly forgotten all about her cat.

But now Amber's half-quirked smile grew to a full grin. "Not surprising he's in the thick of the action. Yup, I'll get him. Thanks, Tabby." She headed out of the room before I could say another word, like she knew exactly where to find that cat. At the very least, Alex knew Hunch was there and could point Amber in the right direction.

By the time we had all the food and supplies stowed away, Amber reappeared with what looked like a suit jacket slung over her arm. "Alex was too busy to talk. He'll catch us up tomorrow, but in the meantime, maybe this little stowaway has learned something important." She opened the suit jacket into the cab of the van and out hopped Hunch, looking annoyed by the whole covert operation.

Amber didn't seem to notice his bad mood, ducking her face close to his and saying, "You'll tell us everything you learned in your investigation, won't you, Hunchie?" It made me wonder if they could hear their cat talk, the way I could hear Sherlock talk back in Crystal Cove.

But Amber didn't wait for a response the way I would have. She kissed the cat on the top of his annoyed forehead, and backed toward where she'd parked her car—on the cleared part of the roundabout driveway, right behind the catering van.

"You'll be over in the morning?" Mallory asked her as she headed out. "Or do you have to be at the station?"

Amber shrugged. "I guess that's up to Detective Martinez, isn't it?"

Mallory watched her go and then got into the driver's seat. I got in, too, with Hunch between us. He lay down with his head on his front paws, looking like he was in focused concentration.

Back at Mallory's house, no sooner did she have the door open when Hunch darted inside past our feet.

"He must be hungry," I guessed, as Mallory and I each lifted a bin of food to bring inside.

"More likely, he's on the case," she told me, in what I thought was a joking tone. But as I wondered what on earth that cat thought he could figure out about the case of a dead man in a hot tub in Mallory's house, we both paused as we passed the living room, where Hunch was almost frantically sniffing at the blue velvet tree skirt.

"What is it Hunch?" Mallory asked him. "Has someone else been in here?"

My blood went cold at the thought. Did she think someone had broken in while we were out?

But that thought had barely made it through my mind when she turned to me and said, "That spice grinder. It's too coincidental that the Petersons had the exact same kind. I don't think it was a treasure hunt from Alex or Amber. I think someone else planted it under my Christmas tree."

"But why?" I asked.

"That's the question, isn't it?" She led the way to the kitchen to set down her bin. I followed. Then she pulled out her phone. "I'm going to text Alex, just to confirm he had nothing to do with the strange gift. I'm sure in the midst of investigating the death of Melvin Peterson, he doesn't have time to come over and take any fingerprints, but let's stay out of the living room for now, just in case." She looked me up and down. "You must be exhausted, Tabby."

I hadn't noticed it until she said the words, but quite suddenly I felt as though I could barely stand. The time difference between Crystal Cove, Oregon and Honeysuckle Grove, West Virginia was three hours, and I'd thought I'd gotten over it, but apparently I had not.

"There's not much to put away, and the stuff outside can wait until morning. Go get some sleep," she told me, and I didn't fight her on it. At this point I wondered if I had enough energy to climb the stairs.

ele

By morning, I felt rejuvenated, however I slept until after ten, which I never, ever, did at home. I had a new text from my sister Pepper. She had been working double shifts all through the holidays and must have texted me late last night.

I texted her back, giving her a quick rundown of the night we'd had catering the Petersons post-Christmas party.

Me: I helped Mallory and Amber cater a Christmas party at an elaborate mansion last night. In the middle of the party, the woman who'd hired them found her father-in-law dead in the upstairs hot tub.

I didn't expect her to be awake, as it was much earlier on the West Coast, but Pepper's response came instantly.

Pepper: Oh no! Did someone kill him? And during the party?

I started to chuckle, but then caught myself. This didn't feel like a situation worth chuckling over. For a second, her words even gave me pause. But then I decided it was only because we were used to solving murder investigations together.

I wrote back, telling her it was nothing like that and not to worry. I thought about calling to reassure her, but then I swore I heard voices coming from downstairs. I wondered how long Mallory had been up and who she was talking to. Was I being rude, sleeping so late?

I quickly brushed my teeth and hair, threw on some jeans and a sweater, and headed for the stairs. Sure enough,

I had heard voices. Three of them, apparently. Amber, Mallory, and Alex were all huddled around the kitchen table speaking quietly.

They went silent as I entered. "Oh, I don't mean to interrupt," I said, taking a step backward to the door.

Mallory and Amber both stared at Alex and before I could leave the room, he said, "No, no, Tabby. Stay. You might be of some help in figuring out what we're missing."

Mallory and Amber immediately brightened. It was like with me and Jay back home. He was in charge, and so I couldn't very well share investigative details, even with Pepper, until clearing it with him, but once I had the okay, I was more than happy to get my intuitive sister's input.

"Coffee's on." Mallory pointed across to her coffee pot. I opened my mouth to offer to make specialty coffees, or at the very least a mocha for Amber, but then quickly shut it again. Now wasn't the time to have a loud espresso maker running.

Seconds later, I had my coffee fixed up and Mallory motioned to a chair between her and Amber. There were mini muffins on a plate in the center of the table and my stomach let out a loud grumble as I sat.

"Lemon cranberry muffin?" Mallory asked, offering the plate toward me. "Amber made them."

I smiled and helped myself to one. When I took my first bite, it burst with juiciness in my mouth. It was so distractingly delicious, I almost missed the recap Alex was giving me.

"The forensics team was at the Peterson's until late last night. We were right about the ground fault circuit interrupter malfunctioning." He looked to Mallory for a second. "It was definitely part of the issue that caused the electrocution."

"Part of the problem?" I asked, immediately switching to my investigative self, the one that didn't hesitate to ask questions.

"The other part was a leak within the pump," Alex told me.

I nodded. "So Mr. Peterson was right in suggesting that the age of the tub was at fault here?"

His face puckered. "That's the thing. We don't think so."

I waited for him to go on, but it was Amber who filled me in. "Both the GFCI and the pump looked as though they could have been tampered with."

I pulled back, immediately recalling Pepper's question for me via text. Did someone kill him? "What are you saying?"

"We're not saying anything yet." Alex pressed his hands flat toward the floor, as if encouraging Amber to calm down. "But we are investigating further. In the meantime, I'm over here trying to get a vibe about the party last night and what impressions you got from Melvin Peterson's family members."

"Well...have you talked about Cindra?" I asked, looking between Mallory and

Amber. Amber looked away, and I wondered if I'd hit a sore spot, bringing her former classmate into this investigation. Still, it was in my nature, or at least it had been drilled into me, to be fully honest. "When I saw the life preserver had been removed from holding Melvin's head above water," I explained, "I immediately thought of Cindra because she had made the comment that her grandfather had wanted to go quickly. He hadn't wanted to suffer."

I offered an apologetic look toward Amber, but now she looked down at her lap, where I noticed she had Hunch snuggled up to her.

"It sounds like the old man had spoken about his own death a lot," Alex observed, helping himself to a muffin. I nodded and took that as my cue to take one more for myself. They were small but delicious.

It seemed like Mallory and Amber had already shared their thoughts with Alex this morning and now they were just waiting on my input. I wished I'd gotten up earlier, so I could have heard their versions. "Mr. Peterson really didn't seem surprised or upset by his father's sudden passing," I told him. "Emily Peterson appeared outwardly upset, but then it seemed her emotions could change on a dime as she put up a cheery façade in front of her guests. In fact, the only one who had seemed truly upset by it was their chef, Victoria."

Alex made a note, and because I didn't know for sure if he knew who I was talking about, I explained.

"She was the one who was sobbing. She was wearing her nightgown, and Cindra, the granddaughter ended up pulling her away. Melvin Peterson had been disgruntled over the fact that Victoria hadn't been preparing the food for last night's party, and it was why he headed up for the hot tub. In fact, it seemed to me like Victoria was the only one on good terms with the old man."

Alex raised his eyebrows. "Tell me more. Who was not on good terms with him."

I felt an urge to pull out my phone to create a new spreadsheet as I tried to recall everyone I'd met the night before. "Well, Mr. Peterson barely reacted to his own father's death. His wife, Emily Peterson, had hired us without telling Melvin, and she definitely seemed to have ruffled the man's feathers by taking it upon herself to hire Mallory and Amber. Cindra didn't care for Emily, her step-mother, but I couldn't really get a read on how she felt about her grandfather." I glanced at Amber, but either she didn't have an opinion, or she had already shared hers. "Then there were a few of the guests. Some thought Melvin Peterson was rude for spending his own party locked away in his hot tub. Others thought it was better not to have his grumbly personality around."

Alex nodded, making notes on his yellow notepad. "Do you have any specific names?"

I thought back. "Only first names. There was Pete and his wife Rosie. They were both complaining about Melvin spending the night being antisocial in the hot tub. Then there were Jerry and

Jenny, husband and wife, and Jerry said something interesting, now that I think about it." All three of them stared at me from around the table, waiting with bated breath. "I guess he's a mechanic of some kind, and he'd been over to fix the hot tub this week."

"Jerry McDonald," Mallory put in. "I saw him at the table."

Alex nodded, still writing. "He works as a technician down at Princeton Pools downtown." The thing about small towns was that if you got enough people in on a discussion, it seemed that someone would always be able to fill in extra details. Alex looked at me. "You're sure he said that? That he'd fixed the hot tub this week? Do you know what day?"

"I'm sure he said he fixed it, and Conrad Peterson mentioned it as well, but I couldn't tell you what day. It didn't sound like it had been in the last couple of days, anyway," I said.

Alex pursed his lips. "Mr. Peterson said his father went in there every night. I'll have to double check on the repair date, and why Jerry was called in. I'll also have to confirm that Melvin Peterson had been in the tub other times since the repair."

"That housekeeper of theirs didn't like Melvin much either," Amber said, nudging the muffin plate first toward Alex and then toward me. We both didn't hesitate to take another.

"I think her name was Rhonda," Mallory put in. "What did she say that made you think she didn't like Melvin?"

"I heard her mumble something to one of the guests. Something about the old man, who I assume is Melvin, only giving his favorite employees the night off."

"Like Victoria," I put in.

"But he didn't give her the night off, remember?" Mallory asked. "It was Emily Peterson who hired us and gave her the night off, and all without Melvin's knowledge."

"And apparently without the rest of the staff's knowledge," Amber said. So it would make sense if Rhonda was perturbed at both Melvin and Victoria."

As we spoke, Alex wrote more notes on a yellow legal pad and drew arrows from some of his notes to other ones. I personally thought my spreadsheets were a more organized method, but who was I to tell a detective how to investigate?

He pushed out his chair and flipped his folder shut over his notes. "Okay, well you've given me lots to go on to get a start on this. Thank you, ladies." He looked to Amber. "Are you coming into the station today?"

She nodded, eagerly. "For sure, if you think I can help."

"I always think you can help, Amber, but especially now. We already had so much to handle over the holidays. Now we really need all hands on deck."

"Can I do anything?" Mallory asked.

Alex shook his head. "You've got a houseguest." She looked a little forlorn at Alex's answer, but he didn't seem to notice and added, "Which reminds me..." He turned to me. "Thank you, Tabby. I wish we could have met under better circumstances, and I hope we haven't ruined your holiday."

He was kind to say so, but I had to tell him the truth. "Honestly, Alex, I'm happy to help in any way I can. I won't be able to think about anything else until this case is solved, so please let us know if there is anything at all we can do."

Alex looked appreciative for the offer, but it seemed he didn't have any jobs for us at the moment. He turned to head for the door, but before he could get there, the spice grinder, which Mallory had left on the back of the kitchen counter, caught my eye.

"Hey, hang on you two." By the time Alex and Amber had turned around, I had the grinder in my hand. For a brief second, I thought maybe I shouldn't be touching it, just in case there really was something suspicious about it, but Mallory and I had both handled the thing so much while we thought it was a treasure hunt clue, it couldn't possibly matter now.

Alex's forehead creased at the grinder, and then up at my face. There was no recognition that I could see. Thankfully, Mallory jumped in to take over the conversation, because she knew them both a lot better than I did.

"We haven't had much time to talk since Christmas," she started. "I found this wrapped up in a gift box under my tree." She took the grinder from me and pulled the typewritten note from the back of the counter. "This note was inside, and at first I figured it was from Tabby. When she said it wasn't, I figured it had to be from one of you. I thought maybe it was a distraction to keep me from getting lonely, or a hint at a bigger gift, but you both knew I already had spice grinders that I was happy with. Then I had the idea that one or both of you had wanted to launch us into a Christmas treasure hunt."

Mallory went on. "It was the only thing that made sense, so we searched far and wide around town for similar spice grinders and how they could lead to our next clue."

She left a pause so long that I couldn't help filling the silence. The suspense was killing me. "We didn't come up with a single lead until last night at the Petersons." Their eyes were all on me. "They had a whole set of these exact same grinders."

Mallory turned it over. "They're not common. We only found similar ones in one store, but they weren't exactly the same. We didn't see any that were exactly the same until Tabby went through the cupboards looking for salt and pepper last night."

I felt my face warm, even though she had asked me to go searching through cupboards.

"If both of you really had nothing to do with giving me this spice grinder, who wrapped it up and put it under my tree?"

Chapter Twelve - Mallory

AT MY WORDS, ALEX and Amber both rushed back toward me, staring at the spice grinder but not taking it from me.

"We fingered it up pretty good while we thought it was a game from one of you. You won't get any prints off of it," I explained, because they looked afraid to touch it.

"Are you saying you think someone has been in your house, Mal?" Alex asked, finally reaching for the spice grinder, but leaving his hands on mine for an extra moment before taking it. The comforting move almost brought tears to my eyes. The last twenty-four hours had been so stressful, with new concerns hitting us at every turn.

"I think so."

"I'm going to get forensics over here right away to take some prints around the house. Do you still have the wrapping?" He read the note again and then stood straighter, having moved into real detective mode.

"I think it's still in the recycle bin." I headed in that direction. "But we were both touching that and looking for clues, too."

Alex nodded. "Still, dig it out if you can. Forensics will want to see it along with the note. We already have yours and Amber's prints on file, but they'll need to take Tabby's when they get here, to rule out any of her fingerprints."

He gave Tabby an apologetic smile, but she immediately responded with, "Of course."

"But forensics has a lot to work on right now," I argued, knowing Alex was only taking this so seriously because he was worried about me.

"It's non-negotiable, Mallory." His thumbs were flying over the texting screen of his phone. "And you might want to put Hunch away. I'll need to get Hunter in here to see if he can pick up a scent." He continued typing into his phone as he headed for his car to retrieve his dog.

His police captain had saddled him with Hunter when he was only a puppy, and forced Alex to drive several hours per week to get the dog trained at the nearest police-dog training unit. It had been an exhausting process, and I'd had to remind myself many times that none of this was Hunter's fault. The result, though, was a proficient-if-overly-friendly dog who had helped with several cases. Hunter and Alex were now a package deal and I loved them both. Hunch, however, had not gotten over his greatest fear: dogs.

And, in fact, the second Alex was out the door, I headed into the living room to find Hunch still sniffing the same spot of the tree skirt he had been sniffing last night. I said the two words I knew would send him running. "Hunter's coming."

Hunch's eyes darted up toward me. There was a pause of maybe two seconds where I saw this information register on his tiny face, and then he tore out of the room like it was on fire.

"Watch out for our guest!" I called out to him, but by the time I made it to the kitchen, Tabby was standing back with her hands up like she was under arrest, and Hunch was already on top of the fridge, his fur pricked out in every direction.

"I'm guessing Hunch doesn't like whoever this Hunter guy is?" Tabby guessed.

I didn't have time to answer her, as a loud WOOF sounded from the entry way.

"Hunter!" Amber's loud coo's sounded from down the hall, and I could see the betrayal all over Hunch's face. I was torn between staying and trying to comfort my cat, and going to say hello to the dog myself.

In only a second, I decided Hunch wouldn't take any comfort from me anyway. He was in protective mode, and would probably be best if we all just left him on his own to calm down a little.

"Do you like dogs?" I asked Tabby. At her nod, I said, "Come on. I'll introduce you."

As soon as we were out of the kitchen, Hunter smelled someone new and leaped toward Tabby. Thankfully, Alex had him on a short leash and the dog almost strangled himself doing it. Alex hadn't put Hunter's police vest on him yet, so he was still in friendly-puppy mode.

"I thought I'd introduce him to Tabby quickly first, so he won't be distracted," Alex explained.

Tabby seemed comfortable with dogs and walked toward Hunter with an open palm outstretched toward him. As usual, when in puppy mode, Hunter licked and slobbered all over Tabby's hand, only trying to get closer so he could show her some love.

She ran her slobbery hand over his head, and he lapped up the attention. Amber continued to stroke his ears, which he loved, and I went over to say hello as well, but decided to keep my distance, as Hunch even had trouble forgiving Amber when she smelled like dog. He had no patience at all for my betrayals.

"Alright, Hunter. It's time to work." Alex pulled out the police-dog vest and Hunter saw it and straightened to a standstill. It was really entertaining watching the transformation of this dog. Alex slipped the vest around him and instructed, "We're looking for an unfamiliar scent, boy. See what you can find."

As he unhooked Hunter's leash, Tabby opened her mouth, like she was going to say something, but only a second later, Hunter sniffed at the front door, at the entryway by the shoes, and soon he seemed to follow a scent straight to where Hunch had been sniffing in the living room. I looked back to Tabby, whose eyes were now wide with awe.

"That's exactly where Hunch was sniffing," I told Alex.

Alex nodded. "Good boy, Hunter. That's the scent we're looking for."

When he finished sniffing around the tree, he headed back to the hallway, but surprisingly, turned away from the front door. As he made his way down the hall, a sense of violation came over me. Had someone been wandering through my house? Had they been upstairs?

But thankfully, Hunter bypassed the stairwell and headed for the kitchen. Hunch would not be happy, but I was curious. If the person had left a spice grinder, had they taken something from my kitchen?

But when we followed Hunter through the kitchen door, he followed the scent straight for the sliding glass door that led to the backyard. He sniffed from the bottom of the door up to the latch, then turned and sat back on his haunches. At the sudden pause in motion, Hunch felt the need to fill the silence with a loud hiss to make his presence known.

To Hunter's credit, he didn't even react to Hunch's outburst. The dog sat staring up at his master.

"This is the way the intruder went out?" Alex asked the dog. Hunter, of course, did not answer, but Alex moved closer, peering at the door latch, but not touching it.

"When's the last time you used this door?" Alex asked me.

I shook my head. "I haven't. Nobody has. You know we never go out in the backyard in the winter."

Alex turned with a humorless grin on his face. "That's good news, because someone left this unlocked, and I'm betting we won't have any problems finding some fresh prints on here."

Chapter Thirteen – Tabby

ALEX PULLED OUT A pair of latex gloves, slipped one on, and then with one finger slid the latch to the locked position. "Unfortunately, I have to get back to the station, but forensics will be here soon. Keep all the doors locked until they show up."

"Should I stay or head to the station?" Amber asked.

"Why don't you stay and ask Scotty what he needs when he gets here. He'll know where they need your help most."

I wondered if Amber knew how to do things like take fingerprints or search for fibers in carpets. Forensic science was such a technical job. I could never do it, but it wouldn't surprise me at all if Amber had the focus for such a profession.

After Alex bagged up the spice grinder and left, I asked Amber, "How long have you been interning with the forensics department?"

She shrugged. "Officially? Since I started college in September. Their police captain doesn't like me much."

"Doesn't like us much," Mallory put in. "Amber had to jump through a lot of hoops to be allowed to help their very understaffed police department." She sighed, but Amber suppressed a grin.

"Unofficially, I've been helping out for almost a year. Better to ask forgiveness than permission, right, Mal?"

Mallory shook her head and sighed. I got the feeling Amber loved pushing Mallory past her comfort zone in all sorts of areas, but while Mallory acted as though she disliked it, part of me sensed that she also appreciated it.

I rubbed the green sea glass that hung from my neck, wondering if it was my magic that helped me know these things or my own intuition. My sea glass hadn't been changing temperature since I left Crystal Cove. In recent months, I had come to rely on it to give me direction when I was stuck, but I wondered if its special magic only worked within the town limits. The lack of any temperature change left me feeling nervous about relying solely on my own intuition when it seemed we were in a situation that might require some extra insight.

"What kind of classes are you taking in school?" I asked Amber, curious to hear more about her skillset.

She rolled her eyes. "Science and math. Bio, Chemistry. I thought I was done with that stuff after high school."

"But you're good at it," Mallory put in.

Amber wasn't done speaking her mind. "I learn way more on the job, when I'm actually in the lab. The classes, unfortunately, are a formality Captain Corbett won't let me get around."

As she finished talking, a knock sounded at the door. All three of us headed in that direction. I was too curious not to. The second we were out of the kitchen, I heard Hunch's soft jump onto the floor. I had a feeling he wouldn't want to be near any of us, even Amber, for the rest of the day after we'd let a rambunctious dog into the house.

But surprisingly, no sooner had Mallory opened the door when Hunch was right there beside her on his haunches, apparently just as curious as the rest of us.

Scotty Hildebrandt was a clean-shaven man in his forties who wore thick glasses and a serious expression.

"What can I do to help?" Amber asked when he'd barely led his two other forensics officers through the door. As the other two slipped into white jumpsuits with matching shower caps and booties, Scotty surveyed the front entryway and then the living room.

"That's where you found the gift?"

Amber nodded. "Under the tree. Mallory's going to see if she can find the gift wrap in her recycling bin." Amber gave Mallory a nod, and Mallory hesitated, like she didn't want to miss anything. If I knew where she kept her recycling, I would go for her. But before I finished that thought, she headed back for the kitchen.

Amber went on to explain the details of the events, and I was surprised at how precise she was, considering she hadn't been here Christmas morning. But she'd clearly been keeping a good eye on Hunter as he'd been investigating the scent.

"Martinez took the spice grinder?" Scotty confirmed.

"He was going to drop it at the lab as soon as he got to the station."

Scotty nodded with a sigh. "There's no one there anyway. Everyone's out working on different cases today, but Martinez insisted we get to this one first. I get it. He wants you to be safe." He ruffled Amber's hair, and I got the impression she was pretty much the only person he had a soft spot for.

She, however, didn't seem to appreciate the coddling. "We'll be fine, but this was already two days ago. If there are prints to be found, and if this somehow ties into the death at the Petersons, we need to figure it out sooner, rather than later."

Leave it to Amber to act like she was in control of the entire forensics department. But I couldn't deny she was smart and helpful. I could see why anyone would put up with her bit of attitude in exchange for her help.

She led the forensics officers into the living room and pointed to specific sections of carpet.

"And I understand the suspect moved through to another exit?" Scotty asked me.

"That's right." I led the way to the kitchen, and even though we'd touched the kitchen door dozens of times since Christmas Eve, I hesitated and let him push through first with his blue-latex-covered hands.

He stopped to survey both sides of the swinging kitchen door and then followed me over to the sliding glass door which led to the backyard.

By this time, Mallory had found the packaging for the gift. I was surprised to see that she, too, was wearing blue latex gloves.

Scotty bagged up the gift wrap and box, as well as the note, which he didn't give any opinion on, and by the time he was finished, Amber pushed through the door into the kitchen.

"I think they found some good fiber samples in the carpet."

Scotty nodded. "Let's see what your young eyes can find for some fingerprints on that door and this one." He pointed to the kitchen door and then the sliding glass one.

"No one's used that one, so that's our best bet." Amber pointed to the glass door. "Where's your kit?"

After getting the red toolbox Scotty had left inside the front door, Amber opened it on the island and I watched in awe as she clearly knew exactly what she was doing. Even with her "young eyes" she wore a headlamp with a magnifying glass as she dusted both areas thoroughly and then exclaimed loudly and excitedly, "I got another one!" each time she managed to isolate a clear fingerprint. "There are also some black markings on here. Looks like dirt or maybe grease."

"Take a sample," Scotty told her.

Even with her excitement, I knew the truth was that these prints wouldn't help us any unless they happened to match with someone's fingerprints the police already had on file in their database. I was always hesitant to get my hopes up when it came to fingerprints, but still, I freely offered my fingers when Amber pulled out the ink kit. I would help in any way I could.

The fibers in the carpet likely wouldn't tell us much, either. There'd been snow outside, which likely would have tracked inside. But that made me remember something.

"You know, on the 23rd when I arrived, I went to put my own gift under the Christmas tree and my knees got moist. At the time, I'd thought it was only because someone had watered the tree and spilled some water, but maybe not."

Mallory and Amber looked at each other and something unsaid passed between them. Finally, Amber turned to Scotty and explained their silent conversation.

"We were out picking up Tabby at the airport that day. I'll bet whoever it was broke in while we were gone, but heard us pull into the driveway and rushed out the glass door into the backyard."

My breath stilled within me. Had we just missed the intruder, and had no idea?

Scotty nodded, and once Amber was done with the glass door, he slid it open, first studying the level of snow right outside the door, and then walking down the porch steps to study the snow there. We'd had several bouts of snowfall since Christmas Eve, so it seemed unlikely he'd find anything, but a few minutes later, he returned, kicked off his snowy boots, and said, "He went around to the left-hand gate. I can still make out depressions. It makes sense that you wouldn't have seen him if there were no lights on in the back."

Mallory shook her head. "I never use the back lights in the winter."

Scotty took in a breath and let it out in a sigh. "Alright, well, there's not much else we can do here. Keep your doors locked." With that, he headed back toward the front door, gathered his two assistants and headed out. "Amber, you'll join us at the lab?" he asked before he left.

She nodded. "Be right there." As soon as she shut the door behind them, she turned to us. "Why would someone break in to put a wrapped spice grinder under your tree? That's what you need to figure out."

Mallory and I both nodded. I didn't have much faith in figuring this out on my own, especially without any magic from my sea glass. But having a friend I could trust and who wanted to find the answers as much as I did—that was something special. Plus, Mallory was not new to investigative work. Maybe if we put our heads together, we'd come up with something.

Chapter Fourteen - Mallory

AS SOON AS AMBER and the forensics team cleared out, I had an insatiable need to cook. I knew I would appear strange to Tabby, and I really had no explanation for this weird obsession of mine, but I also knew I wouldn't be able to think straight until I got deep into a recipe.

Tabby followed me into the kitchen and watched silently as I shlumped a bag of flour onto the counter beside my giant recipe book from culinary school and then started quickly flipping pages.

"Can you check the freezer," I asked, "and see if there are any frozen blueberries? They should be on the second shelf." I motioned with my head toward my side-by-side fridge and freezer, not meeting her eyes for fear that she'd stop me before I even got going.

I was looking for something specific, but I couldn't even slow down my racing thoughts enough to figure out what. I just knew it had blueberries.

Tabby set a bag of frozen blueberries beside the flour on the counter, looking at me sidelong.

"I have to cook. It helps me think." It was the most explanation I could give her.

Thankfully, she nodded, and said, "I get that. I'm that way sometimes, too—not so much with cooking, but I have my own systems to help me think. Let me know what I can do to help."

Ten minutes later, I'd found the blueberry coffee cake recipe that was skimming my subconscious and Tabby had gathered all the ingredients as I listed them off and told her where to find them.

"Okay, I can take it from here," I told her, finally feeling like I could think properly again. "Once I get going with mixing the ingredients together, I'll be ready to talk about the case. Why don't you grab a pad of paper and a pen from the table and make some notes as we come up with ideas."

Tabby nodded, but she didn't head for the table. Instead, she pulled out her phone. "Actually, I prefer to use a spreadsheet, if that's okay with you? While you have cooking, my spreadsheets help me. They help me keep all the details of a case easier to manage and look at with a glance."

I stared at her. I wouldn't have a clue where to even start in reading a spreadsheet of case ideas, let alone constructing one. But I was certainly willing to learn. I wasn't the only person in the room who had helped to solve murder cases, after all.

I got back to measuring my flour and said, "Absolutely. Whatever works for you, and as long as you can help me relay any of the details to Alex later."

Her thumbs typed into her phone for several minutes, and then finally she started to speak and go over the information we knew so far.

"Someone broke into your house, probably on December 23rd, and left quickly when we arrived back here from the airport. They left a wrapped spice grinder that matches exactly with a set of spice grinders in the Peterson's home. Do you remember the gifts wrapped up under their tree?"

I tried to think back and shook my head.

"I'm pretty sure some of them were silver. It would be good to check if the gift wrap had a similar pattern to the one we found under your tree. Melvin Peterson died in that same home on December 26th, three days later, and it appears that the hot tub he died in had been tampered with. Cindra Peterson may have had compassion for her grandfather and wanted to grant his wish of a quick death, rather than suffering for months or years. She may have removed the life preserver from under him. We should ask Alex if he would question her about that."

I nodded, and as I thought about this, I let my mind go even further on this train of thought. "What if she did more than remove the life preserver?" Tabby looked at me blankly, so I explained. "She knows her trades well. If someone tampered with the electrical outlet, could it have been her?"

Tabby pursed her lips. "But would electrocution have been a painless choice, if she had done it out of compassion? And we think she removed the life preserver because she was the only person upstairs who knew about him in there, and anyone could have done it, but would she have really known how to rig the hot tub outlet in order to electrocute him?"

I shrugged. "From what I've heard she knows that and a lot more." I set my cold butter into a glass dish and placed it into some hot water in the sink to soften it quickly. All the while, my mind was turning, trying to go back to what Alex had mentioned last night about Cindra.

"Remember how Amber said that Cindra was a bit of a snob?" At Tabby's nod, I went on. "At first, I couldn't see it. Cindra didn't seem like the wealthy type who would look down on others, and even if she did, as far as Amber's classmates knew, Amber also came from a wealthy part of town." I measured out the cinnamon, sugar, and salt, and mixed them into the flour. "Alex indicated that the reason Amber and Cindra didn't get along was because Cindra was deep into the trades program at school and she didn't have a lot of patience for anyone who took up space, just taking one trades course and then taking all of the teacher's attention because of their lack of skill."

"Didn't Amber also say Cindra was highly competitive?" Tabby typed this into her phone, without looking up for my agreement. "So you're saying Cindra may well have had the skill to mess with the hot tub wiring?"

"It's definitely possible. And as for your other question, to my knowledge, electrocution is very painful. The electric current produces involuntary muscle contractions, burns, and ultimately cardiac arrest. We saw evidence of the burns on Melvin Peterson's back. Cindra would have had to have seen that, too, and she didn't seem regretful or tormented about it, did she?"

Tabby shook her head. "What if the compassion was an act? I'd like to talk to Cindra more, now that we know foul play was involved. Do you think Amber could set up a meeting for us? And do you think that would be okay with Alex?"

"I'm sure Alex would be in favor of the help. I'm not sure about his captain, though, so we may have to keep any meetings under the radar for the moment." I started on a separate bowl of wet ingredients. "I'll text Alex and Amber as soon as I get this mixed."

Tabby sat at a kitchen chair and nibbled her lip. "Back to the spice grinder. Let's say Cindra did electrocute her grandfather. Why would she have wrapped up a spice grinder and broken into your house to leave it under your Christmas tree? What reason could she possibly have for wanting you to be suspicious of the goings on at her house?"

I squinted as I whisked the eggs. "Could someone have known that Cindra planned to kill her grandfather, and wanted to tip us off?" It still didn't make sense, and Tabby said so.

"But what does a spice grinder have to do with an old man getting electrocuted in a hot tub?"

I sighed. "I wish I knew." As I reached for the cinnamon again, a thought occurred to me. "Who uses spice grinders?"

"Anyone could," Tabby said, looking at me like she wasn't following. "For all we know, they put the salt and pepper ones out on the table each night for dinner."

"But the specialty ones, like saffron…?" I turned to face her. "Only a chef would use something like that."

"Or maybe Mrs. Peterson, if she ever cooks," Tabby said, poking holes into my theory, like Amber usually did.

I shook my head. "Mrs. Peterson doesn't seem the type. She didn't want to have anything to do with the food last night. She just wanted us to prepare and serve everything, and she didn't even seem to want to taste anything." I shook my head again. "She's not a foodie, or a cook, in my opinion."

Tabby nodded, typing into her phone again. "Right, so Victoria, the chef, who was wildly upset over Melvin's death?

You think she had something to do with it?"

I did not think that, and so I focused my thoughts elsewhere. "The note inside said something about a towel closet. There was a free-standing towel closet in the solarium. Perhaps they should take fingerprints of that?"

Tabby's face brightened, like this was all making some kind of sense. And maybe it was. I pulled the softened butter out of the sink so I could wash my hands. "I'm texting Alex with my thoughts right now. I'll also text Amber to see if she can get us not only a meeting with Cindra, but let's see if she'll bring Victoria along, too. Somebody has to know something about the spice grinder we found under the tree."

Chapter Fifteen - Tabby

BETWEEN MALLORY, AMBER, AND Alex, they came up with a plan: Amber would text Cindra, indicating we had a possible cooking job for Victoria, and we'd like to meet with her under the radar of the rest of her family.

We were taking a chance, but we all had the sense that Cindra wasn't hugely allegiant to her parents, and in fact, would revel at the opportunity to rebel against them.

We were right.

I had just gotten out of the shower and gotten dressed when Mallory called, "I heard back from Amber!"

I raced downstairs, still towel drying my hair. "What did she say?"

Mallory showed me her phone screen.

Amber: Cindra texted back. Will paste below.

"Her text is followed by a thumbs-up emoji, which seems like good news, but I've been waiting for her second one to come through." Mallory's words were barely out of her mouth when her phone pinged in her hands.

I read over her shoulder.

Cindra: Dad and Emily are at the funeral home making arrangements so they gave the staff the day off. It would have to be today and she'll be

at the house all day but I can't be there. Gotta work at the shop all day.

I'd barely looked to Mallory for a reaction when another text from Amber popped up.

Amber: She sent me Victoria's number but I was hoping you and Tabby could talk to them both at once. Do you think Cindra's avoiding us?

"I have an idea," Mallory said and she started typing.

Mallory: Ask Cindra for her place of work and what time she eats. Tell her I'll make her lunch and bring it over if she gets Victoria to meet us there.

Another thumbs-up emoji quickly appeared on Mallory's screen.

"I called Alex while you were in the shower," Mallory told me. "Apparently the forensics team drained the hot tub through the night, and have confirmed very recent tampering with the pump as well."

"Purposeful tampering?" I asked. "They're sure?"

Mallory nodded. "We'll get more details later, after Alex has had time to meet with the forensics investigators. For the moment, though, he's all in favor of us finding a way to get a read on both the chef and the granddaughter."

I liked how Mallory referred to them by their roles, rather than their names. It helped keep the whole investigation in perspective. I sometimes got too close to suspects and then had trouble believing shady motives of anyone.

I pulled up my spreadsheet on my phone and skimmed through all the information I had entered so far. "If Victoria suspected Cindra of foul play, though, and sent us the spice grinder to tip us off, is it a good idea to question them together?" This was the best theory we had come up with so far, but it still didn't sit right with me. I touched my sea glass, willing it to offer some inspiration, but it remained cool in my fingers. All I could hope was that if we followed this through, it might lead to another clue.

Mallory pursed her lips. "If we can get them both to Cindra's 'shop,' wherever that is, we'll see how they're acting together. You watch Victoria, I'll watch Cindra, and if we feel like we need more time with either of them, we'll try to find a way to split them up to delve deeper."

"Should we come up with a code word?" I suggested. "Then, if you use it, I'll walk Victoria out to her car—or you can. Whatever you think."

Mallory's eyes flickered back and forth over mine, and I felt like she could pretty much read my thoughts as she did it. "How about pickles?"

My eyebrows shot up. "Um...okay." I said the word, but I didn't really follow. If one of us suddenly shouted "Pickles!" that would have to look crazy to our two suspects.

But then Mallory clarified. "We'll make up something with pickles for lunch. If one of us wants to get one of our suspects alone, we'll ask them if they like pickles. That'll be the cue for the other one to make it happen."

I loved investigating with Mallory. While working with Jay was wonderful, it always felt uneven, since he's a professional and I'm not. With Pepper I still had to fight my over-protective side. But Mallory and I were equals in this, and it made me appreciate our friendship even more. She was smart and savvy and I had no doubt we would get to the bottom of this investigation together.

Her phone pinged, and her smile brightened. "Amber says it's a go. We have an address and have to be there by one with something delicious."

———

Mallory and I spent the next two hours first making buns from scratch, and then building them into elaborate sandwiches—with pickles. I was glad to be able to help in the kitchen and even more so when Mallory tasked me with making some sort of wintery coffee treats to bring to each of them. I chose a peppermint mocha with an extra pump of caramel, a specialty I'd come up with at The Heirloom Café in Crystal Cove.

I had the sense that while Cindra seemed tough on the outside, she was the type that would enjoy a decadent sweet coffee. I usually had a pretty good sense of what type of coffee customers would like. I'd always thought that had been a trait inherent from my sea glass, but maybe not, because I felt the same assurance with Cindra now, far from Crystal Cove. While I hadn't spent enough time with Victoria to have been able to read her, I hoped that my special Christmas coffee would suit her just as well.

After packing them into a couple of to-go coffee cups, we headed for the door, only to see Hunch waiting there like he expected to be able to open the front door with his determined focus.

Mallory raised her eyebrow at the cat. "You can come in the van, but I don't know that you'll be allowed into..." She paused to read the name off her phone screen. "Big Rig Machinery."

Whether or not Hunch understood her words, I had no idea, but as Mallory opened her front door, and the cat raced out, it was clear he did not intend to be left behind.

Even though the cat didn't have much interest in communicating with me, he sure made me miss my own cat Sherlock.

Chapter Sixteen - Mallory

BIG RIG MACHINERY WAS not far out of town on the main highway. It was still five to one, and so we sat in the parking lot for a few minutes with the heat pumping in the catering van to keep us warm.

From the outside, it looked like a large mustard-yellow warehouse. There were a few tractors parked out near the edge of the highway in the snow. I wondered if those were items they sold or had repaired, or if they were just sitting out on the highway's edge as advertisements for their business.

Tabby seemed to have many of the same questions. "Do you think Cindra works as a tractor salesperson?"

I thought back to the night before, nibbling my lip. "Her fingernails were caked with grease. I'm thinking she's more likely a repairperson."

"Like a mechanic?"

Hunch's head volleyed back and forth from between us on the bench seat as each of us spoke, but now he kept his gaze on Tabby, as though he could sense she was putting something together.

Cindra was young, but the impression I'd gotten from Amber over muffins this morning was that she knew pretty much everything there was to know about building, mechanics, and electrical back in tenth grade. "That's what I'm thinking."

"Didn't Amber and that forensics officer notice grease on your sliding glass door latch?" Tabby asked.

My eyes widened. "They said it could have been dirt." My suggestion was no more than half-hearted. I was trying to find the holes in this theory, perhaps because Cindra was so young, but in truth, this did seem like an important clue.

Before we could discuss this any further, a nineties model Volkswagen hatchback pulled into the lot beside us, about four car spaces away. Victoria sat behind the steering wheel and stared up at the building, and didn't seem to notice us. She wiped at her eyes with a tissue.

"Could she truly be playing up the emotion for our benefit?" Tabby murmured. "If so, she's a great actress."

Exactly what I was thinking. "Even better than Emily Peterson."

Victoria heaved in a big breath and let it out before reaching for the door handle. I instantly reached for mine. "Shall we get a few minutes with her on the walk in?"

Tabby read my mind. She already had the coffee cups in hand and reached for her own door. Hunch followed me out on my side, but Victoria was already several steps ahead. Even though Hunch hated the snow, I'd have to worry about him in a few minutes.

I yanked out the soft-sided cooler with our lunch from the middle floor and stepped as quickly as I could, practically skating across the plowed parking lot. Tabby was slower, probably not as used to walking on ice and snow, and also carrying hot drinks, so this was up to me to catch up.

"Victoria?" I called.

She slowed and turned around. Her eyes were red. Could this truly be acting? Did she put some drops in to redden her eyes before arriving?

"Hi, I'm Mallory," I said, quickly catching up. "We didn't get a chance to meet last night, and I'm so sorry about the turn of events."

She shook her head almost violently. "I can't talk about that. I thought you wanted to tell me about a job."

I tried to offer a comforting smile. "I did. I do," I corrected. "Let's get inside where it's warm and I'll tell you all about it."

Tabby caught up and outstretched one of the coffee cups. "Here. This should help you warm up."

Victoria hesitated, but then took the drink from Tabby. She didn't immediately take a sip, and instead started walking toward the building again.

She opened the single glass door first and walked through as though this wasn't the first time she had been here. I let Tabby follow and then put a finger to my lips toward Hunch before letting him into the entryway. Even though there was a counter with a cash register behind it in the small rundown lobby, there was no one manning it at the moment.

Hunch moved inside and immediately started sniffing at every square inch of the floor. That cat was more doglike than catlike, but I had to admit, his keen sense of smell had helped us to solve investigations more than once in the past.

Straight ahead, the lobby opened into the main warehouse, where there was a whirring sound, like a drill or an electric saw of some kind. We had only just entered the warehouse when the whirring sound stopped. I followed it to where Cindra stood behind a large wooden work table. She wore protective eyewear and held a drill in one hand and she appeared to be working on some kind of complicated pulley system. I wondered which piece of large equipment throughout the warehouse it belonged to. There were not only tractors and cranes and excavators in the open, triple-story warehouse, but washing machines and standalone motors and even what looked like commercial sized computers.

Cindra put down her drill, slid up her eyewear, and checked her watch. Then she strode toward us. "Thanks for being on time. They don't let me take my lunch until they're back at one." She motioned for us to follow her then strode toward a wooden stairway that led up to a second floor that only covered maybe an eighth of the large warehouse. When we reached the top of the stairs, in a big open room, five greasy, burly looking men were throwing their refuse into a giant garbage can and going back to work.

The men looked over us on their way out of the room, making me suddenly feel very prissy and out of place, but Cindra told them, "It's okay, they're with me." The men grunted their replies and didn't say another word about it.

"They're letting me apprentice here," Cindra explained as soon as they were out of earshot. "I figured they wouldn't care if I had visitors during my lunch break, but I guess I'll have to bring donuts tomorrow to make up for it."

The men hadn't looked upset, or even really like they cared, but then Cindra knew them better than I did.

She motioned to a table in the middle of the room. All the white Formica tables were smudged with grease, but this middle table at least looked the cleanest from crumbs. I was tempted to go to the nearby counter and grab a rag to wipe it, but one glance at the sink told me any rags I'd find around this place would be equally greasy.

"Did you already tell her about the job?" Cindra asked as she sat. Tabby passed her the other coffee and Cindra took a sip before registering the flavor and then saying, "Thanks. This is really good." There was very little emotion in Cindra's voice, but in the short time I had heard her talk, I really hadn't heard much in the way of emotion from her, even over her dead grandfather.

Victoria finally took a sip of her coffee, tentatively, like she thought we'd poisoned it or something.

I pulled out the sandwiches and passed them out to all four of us. "We have a big catering job coming up on January fifteenth and could use an extra set of competent hands." This was true. Amber would be super busy between school and the forensics lab. I didn't know for sure if I wanted Victoria to be the one to help me, as I didn't even know her skill level, but I had written up an advertisement looking for someone. I just hadn't posted it yet.

Victoria wiped her eyes again as a new round of tears had streamed out since we'd come inside the building. "Oh. You mean it's only for a one-time event?"

I didn't want this lunch appointment to be over before it had even started, so I said, "Maybe not. If it works out, we could certainly use you for more events."

Victoria looked between me and Tabby, incorrectly assuming this was the "we" I was referring to. It didn't seem worth mentioning right now that Amber, my teenage associate, would also have to approve her involvement.

"I really need a full time job." Victoria blew her nose. I had a hard time believing she would be able to apply for any kind of job in her current state, let alone make specific demands.

Cindra explained further before I could say anything. "Her boyfriend hurt his back and has been out of work for almost a year. She's supporting both of them. Now that Gramps is dead, Victoria knows her days at our house are numbered. Even if Dad wanted to keep her on, he's not going to fight Emily on it. All the house staff will likely be replaced within the month."

This suggestion brought on a new round of tears from Victoria. I did feel bad for the girl. She couldn't have been more than twenty-five, probably fresh out of culinary school, and probably now wouldn't have any decent references to be able to show to prospective new employers. It could be difficult to get employment in restaurants, and even as a fully accredited chef, a person often had to work their way up the ranks.

But Cindra's explanation brought on another thought: Victoria seemed to be one of the only people Melvin Peterson liked. Could she have been listed in his will? Her desperation for money could have given her motive.

"Well, I can't promise you full time," or any work at all before talking to Amber, I added silently, "but if the Petersons do let you go, we can see what we can offer you to tide you over. At the very least, maybe you'll end up with a good reference." Again, that was a big maybe, as I had no idea about her competence, not to mention that, from everything we had learned, she was a murder suspect at the moment. "How long have you worked for the Petersons?"

"For almost two years," Cindra said, speaking for her again. "Grandpa met her at some foodie trade show and brought her home to cook for us."

Interesting. I had cooked a trade show once when I was barely out of culinary school. It was not a pleasant employment opportunity—long hours with very little appreciation. I'd be willing to bet she was pretty happy to have gotten the job offer from the senior Mr. Peterson.

"It was so strange that Mrs. Peterson gave me last night off. Melvin usually bragged about my food to any guests," Victoria said, sniffling with her words.

"Were you angry when Emily Peterson told you that you wouldn't be cooking for their big party?" Tabby asked.

"Angry? No, of course not. It's a great job, and I appreciate it. It was actually nice to have a night off." I wasn't entirely sure if this was true or if she was saying this so she appeared employable. "Did you have another chef before Victoria?" I asked Cindra, hoping I wasn't treading too far off topic. Cindra seemed like the kind of girl that might call a person on something like that.

But thankfully, she didn't seem to notice. "Yeah. We've always had a cook of some kind, except when I was about ten and we were between kitchen help, and Rhonda filled in for a while." She made a face like she'd just spooned a large hunk of dirt into her mouth.

I had to bite back my smile.

"Your parents don't spend much time in the kitchen?" Tabby asked. I liked her way of thinking. Maybe we could narrow down who would have spent time around those spice grinders.

Cindra balked. "Are you kidding? That would be worse than Rhonda. And Emily is not my parent," she added.

Right. I'd have to be careful not to make that mistake again. "So Victoria has that big beautiful kitchen all to herself, all the time?" I asked, like I was just making a general complimentary observation.

"These days, yeah." Cindra looked at Victoria, whose tears had finally started to dry up. "But remember when Marissa was still around? It seemed like a tornado hit the kitchen every time the two of them came over and wanted to show off a new recipe they'd copied off Master Chef." I wondered who "the two of them" were, but one thing was clear: Cindra was trying to lift Victoria's spirits by reminding her of funnier if not happier times. Even though the young girl didn't have a lot in way of emotion when she spoke, it was clear to me in this instant that she cared about Victoria. It must have been why she had been the one to rush off to break the news to her about her grandpa last night.

I considered again if the two young women could have conspired to kill the old man. Cindra, I could tell, would have been the one to set this in motion—in an effort to ease her grandfather's suffering, and perhaps even to get

Victoria a financial settlement from his will. Victoria could be covering her involvement with her heavy displays of emotions.

"Tell me about what kinds of cooking you specialize in," I said to Victoria, figuring I'd better get back to my supposed reason for being here before Cindra called me on it.

Victoria took a bite of her sandwich as she seemed to consider her answer. She chewed several times and swallowed. I waited for her to comment on the flavor. Our own version of a Monte Cristo always got rave reviews from clients—especially in the wintertime.

"Mr. and Mrs. Peterson generally eat keto, so I've learned to slow cook a lot of beef and chicken and dress it up with avocado-based salads. Cindra and the senior Mr.... Mr..." She sobbed into her hands.

Cindra took over. "We would go through pasta like it was our last meal." She didn't seem to notice the irony of this statement. I continued to study Victoria as she took another bite as though the food might relieve her tears. As she chewed and chewed and wiped her eyes, it looked like she was barely tasting the sandwich.

If she'd had anything to do with her boss's death, she was an exceptional actress.

"Do you ever add pickles?" Tabby asked. My gaze snapped to her. Sure, we'd had a code word planned out, but I thought she'd be a little more discreet with it. Just as I turned back to Victoria to try and add a segue before anyone noticed this strange change of subject, Tabby spoke again, seemingly ready with her own plan. "I've heard a lot of people who are on ketogenic diets really like the strong flavor of garlic dills."

She was asking Victoria, so she must have something further she'd like to ask her on her own. I didn't mind this one bit, because I would love to have five minutes alone with Cindra.

Chapter Seventeen - Tabby

VICTORIA WAS ON HER last bite within minutes. It was as if she was using her large sandwich to stanch the tears in her throat. I was worried that Cindra would suddenly claim to have to go back to work, even though we'd only been in here for ten minutes.

Apparently, Cindra wouldn't be the problem, though.

Victoria pushed back her chair and stood. "I should probably go. Cindra can give you my number, and you can text me if you have an event you need help with. But if it conflicts with my work for the Petersons, I won't be able to do it."

Somehow in the last ten minutes, she had decided she wasn't getting fired. But by the raised eyebrow Cindra gave to this statement, I had a feeling she wasn't as confident in the permanence of Victoria's job. And I had a feeling Cindra knew about these things better than Victoria did.

Regardless, I wanted to press Victoria further with a few more pointed questions, especially about the spice grinders, as it seemed she was the only one to spend any time with them. I stood, too. "I'll walk you out. I need to go out and check on our cat, anyway." It was the only excuse I could come up with on short notice, even though I doubted I'd be able to locate Hunch, and even if I did, he likely wouldn't let me near him.

But thankfully Victoria didn't seem to have a problem with this.

Cindra asked, "Cat? You brought your cat?" And I rushed out of the room after Victoria, having a lot more confidence that Mallory could come up with an excuse about this better than I could.

Victoria and I were outside the lunchroom and on the wooden stairs before I spoke again. Unfortunately, now I had to speak over some loud equipment clunking and whirring from within the warehouse.

"I was admiring the Petersons' spice grinders when I was working in their kitchen last night," I practically yelled.

She nodded. "I think they're pretty expensive. Everything in the Petersons' house is."

We moved into the lobby at the bottom of the stairs and I closed the door behind us so it would be quieter. There was a glass window on the door, and one of the burly men stopped what he was doing and watched us, but thankfully, he didn't follow us out.

I watched Victoria carefully as I asked my next question. "I bet they even have one of those grinders filled with saffron then, huh?"

Victoria nodded, but showed no obvious reaction as she said, "Mr. Peterson keeps the saffron on the dining room table. He adds it to everything." She dropped to just above a whisper as she added, "It only really releases its flavor with heat, but I think it makes him think it takes his meals up a level."

"Conrad Peterson?" I confirmed. I thought back to whether or not there had been a spice grinder on the dining room table. I'd been so busy serving each time I was in the dining room, I couldn't be sure. At Victoria's nod, I asked, "When was the last time you saw that saffron grinder?"

I feared I may have been too obvious with my question, but Victoria didn't seem to notice. "It ran out the other day. Rhonda does the grocery shopping, so I added it to her list. I assumed she took it to refill it, but Conrad has been asking about it all week."

Interesting. I was eager to mark these new developments into my spreadsheet. Their saffron grinder was missing. One of the same turned up under Mallory's Christmas tree. What were the chances that these were two different grinders? Not much, I had to guess. Would Conrad have been asking after the saffron if he had something to do with sending the grinder our way? Likely not.

Victoria turned toward the door and hesitated when she saw it was snowing again. I had to get onto my next subject before she left.

"It seems like you had a special relationship with Melvin," I said.

For the first time, Victoria didn't launch into hysterics at the mention of the old man. Perhaps she had cried herself out for the moment. "He changed my life. Thanks to him, I had a real job, and not one in a kitchen surrounded by junkies."

I was surprised at this, and it must have shown, because as she turned back to me, she went on to say. "You must know, if you've worked in any kind of restaurant."

I wasn't sure if I should continue to pretend to be on the local catering circuit with Mallory or not. For the moment, I hedged, saying, "I've been pretty fortunate in all the jobs I've had so far. Definitely nothing like you're talking about."

She shook her head. "It's pretty bad out there. I don't know what I'll do if Emily Peterson fires me."

"Don't you think she'd rather keep good help than have to look for someone new?" I was trying to work my way toward getting her thoughts on the divisiveness between Emily and Melvin.

I figured who better to ask than the only person who seemed to have a serious allegiance to the old man.

Victoria shrugged. "That's the hope, but you never know with that woman."

"She can be erratic?" I guessed.

"That's putting it mildly." Thankfully, now that we were tearing down Emily Peterson, Victoria didn't seem in any hurry to finish this conversation and get out into the cold.

"It didn't seem like she got along with many people," I suggested.

Victoria harrumphed and nodded, but didn't elaborate.

"She really didn't get along with Melvin, huh? I was surprised they could share a house."

Victoria stared out the glass door. I didn't want to go out in the cold weather any more than she did. "Believe me, it was only out of necessity."

"What kind of necessity?" I asked. I wondered if Mallory was getting this much useful information out of Cindra.

Victoria took in a big breath. I hoped she wasn't going to break into tears again, and for the moment she didn't. "Melvin Peterson was really sick. Sometimes, when he wasn't doing well, he needed help getting up the stairs. Just someone to help balance him, and he had a thing about accepting help from strangers or even nurses. I helped whenever I was around, or Cindra, or Conrad, but Emily Peterson...well, she would just sit on the couch and watch him struggle all the way to the top step. I'd heard Melvin talking to his son one time about kicking him and his wife out if she couldn't even help him up the stairs once in a while."

"So Melvin owned the house?" I asked. I didn't know why, but for some reason I had assumed Emily and Conrad owned the house and let the old man live with them.

"Well...yeah," Victoria said the words as though they should have been obvious. Maybe they would have been from someone who had been hired by Melvin at the onset, but it certainly had not seemed obvious to Mallory... or to me for that matter.

"I can't imagine Emily was happy living in a house owned by a man who seemed to hate her." I spit out the observation as I noticed through the door's window one of the burly men headed in our direction. I didn't have Mallory's van keys, but soon we were going to be forced to take this conversation out into the cold.

"Mrs. Peterson was definitely not happy. That's an understatement." Noticing the burly man, Victoria put a hand on the glass door.

"Do you think she hated her situation enough that she wanted the old man dead?" My words came out in a rush, and the second they left my mouth it was clear they were much, too blunt. Victoria's eyes welled up again, and she didn't stick around to respond.

Her words trailed behind her as she pushed out the door. "I can't think about that!"

And I may have gone after her, if not for the burly man and the annoyed cat that was now outstretched in one of his meaty hands.

"Who let a cat into our shop?" he yelled, and his words were directed straight at me.

Chapter Eighteen – Mallory

I HAD JUST GOTTEN Cindra to open up a little about some of the party-goers who hated Melvin Peterson when a man burst into the lunchroom.

"You're going to want to go and get your friend and her cat," he said with clear disdain, "before they freeze to death!"

I stood and reached for my keys all in one motion. We'd finished our sandwiches, and so I scooped up our garbage on my way to the door. "Can I call you to talk more?" I asked Cindra.

But she only shrugged in response, returning to her stoic self, and pushed past me and the big man in the doorway, apparently ready to get back to work without another word.

Since I'd had her talking a surprising amount when no one else was around, I was eager to make notes about our conversation, but the big man crossed his arms over his barrel of a chest and watched me until I followed Cindra down the stairs.

She headed straight to her workstation without so much as a wave goodbye, so I headed for the lobby and then the glass door to find Tabby just outside, under an overhang of the building to keep out of the falling snow. While she had Hunch in her arms, probably for warmth for the both of them, he wore what I could only describe as his special brand of Hunch scorn at needing someone other than Amber.

"I'm so sorry!" I said. "I forgot to give you the keys."

She shook her head and followed me to the van. "I'm fine. I just want to get inside so I can make some notes into my phone."

I wanted her to make notes for me, too, and so I tried to keep everything I'd learned from Cindra straight in my head as I drove and Tabby rattled off bits of information as she typed them into her phone.

"Victoria said that Melvin Peterson actually owns the mansion and lets his son Conrad and wife Emily live there. Apparently, he needed help sometimes, with things like getting up the stairs, and didn't like to depend on strangers. Conrad Peterson and Cindra often helped the man, and so did Victoria, and even the housekeeper Rhonda helped him from time to time, despite the fact that they didn't care much for each other. But apparently Emily Peterson would just sit on the couch and watch him struggle. They hated each other with a passion, and even though I couldn't quite get Victoria to admit as much, I think the woman hated her father-in-law enough to want him dead!"

Tabby finally took a breath. I hadn't really considered Mrs. Peterson as a suspect, but this suddenly made a lot of sense. Then again, so did the information Cindra had told me.

"I got Cindra talking, and, well, can you make a note of the names Pete and Jerry?"

Tabby nodded, typing again. "I remember them from the party. Pete was the redheaded guy with the gorgeous platinum blonde wife, Rosie. And Jerry—wasn't he the mechanic Pete was hanging out with most of the evening? The one who had worked on the hot tub?"

I nodded, taking a turn onto my street and putting my windshield wipers on high to battle the falling snow. "Jerry fixed the hot tub on December 22nd. Apparently, he'd been planning to be off work from the 20th until New Years, but Melvin Peterson had called him and all but demanded he get in that day to fix his hot tub."

"Sounds like Jerry didn't care for the man too much," Tabby observed as she was typing. "Pete had been grumbling about him last night at the party, too. Complaining that he'd rather spend the night in his hot tub than with the people he'd invited over."

"So Melvin had handled the invitations?" I asked. "Not Mrs. Peterson?"

Tabby looked up as I pulled the catering van into my driveway. "It sounded to me like Melvin was in charge of pretty much everything about the party. That's why it seemed like such a deviation that Emily chose to give Victoria the night off and hire you instead."

"So if someone was truly responsible for Melvin Peterson's electrocution, who seems the most likely? The redheaded man who was annoyed at him not showing up to his own party?"

"Right, Pete," Tabby said. "His dad and Melvin were business rivals, and from what I overheard, he always felt like Melvin had cheated his dad out of certain successes. I got the sense there was an implied lack of respect by inviting Pete to the party but not showing up."

I nodded. "That does seem like motive. What about the mechanic whose vacation was ruined by the old man?"

"He's a more likely suspect, in my opinion." Tabby touched the pretty green stone that hung from her neck, a look of consternation on her face as she added, "Apparently, Melvin had refused to pay Jerry properly, but said that he'd tell everyone what a lousy mechanic he was if Jerry pressed him. He was faced with having his Christmas vacation ruined without recompense, and also his job threatened if he did anything about it."

The more I learned, the more there were several people with serious motive. "Then there's the scorned daughter-in-law, who didn't want to be living under the man's constant demands and scrutiny." We had good reason to consider them all suspects.

Then Tabby added, "And have we actually cleared Cindra or Victoria from suspicion?" At my sigh, she said, "I don't get the sense either of them actually did it, especially not Victoria. She truly seems to be in a state of shock and grief over his death, but we have to continue to look at everyone until we know for sure. Right?"

I nodded and reached for Hunch. While he was self-sufficient in most ways, he particularly hated getting his paws cold and wet in the snow. It was likely the only reason he'd put up with Tabby holding him for so long out in the cold.

By the time we got inside, I had a text from Alex.

Alex: New information from forensics. Got time to sift through the file with me?

I texted back immediately.

Me: Tabby and I just got home. Want me to come there or do you want to come to my place?

Alex: Bradley's taking Hunter to the indoor dog park for an hour. Why don't I come there?

After texting my agreement, I turned to Tabby. "Alex's partner is dog-sitting for a while. He's headed over here with new information. Want to help me get something sweet in the oven before he gets here?"

Chapter Nineteen – Tabby

WE SAT AROUND MALLORY'S small kitchen table, eating delicious Chess Pie, which consisted of sweet pie dough filled with cornmeal custard, apparently a West Virginia staple, and something that Mallory knew how to bake without a recipe.

Alex flipped open a file folder and the three of us—Mallory, Hunch, and I—sat forward on our chairs to listen as he read from his notes.

"When I interviewed Mr. and Mrs. Peterson, both seemed convinced that the death was an unfortunate accident. When I introduced the idea of foul play, they were both more concerned about keeping any suggestion of that out of the news than they were about discovering who may have wanted to hurt the old man."

"So you believed them?" Mallory asked.

"The jury is still out in my mind. I wanted to interview them again today, especially Emily, right after I received my report from forensics. As soon as I mentioned electrical tampering, she immediately said her step-daughter Cindra knew all about electrical wiring, but Conrad quickly shut the conversation down and claimed they would be too busy at the funeral home to meet with me again today. We have an appointment at ten in the morning tomorrow."

I could sense Alex's frustration at having to wait, but more importantly, was Emily Peterson only throwing her step-daughter under the bus as a distraction, or did she truly expect Cindra of some wrongdoing? It seemed as if Mr. and Mrs. Peterson were at the heart of this investigation, Alex should be able to demand an interview whenever he wanted. But I wasn't here to tell him how to do his job. Instead, I wanted to catch him up on our notes, so he at least knew they were serious suspects.

"Apparently, Emily and Melvin Peterson really hated each other. Melvin owns the mansion and let his son Conrad, and his wife Emily move in, but Emily would sit and watch the old man struggle in trying to climb the stairs. Everyone else in the household would help, even the housekeeper Rhonda, but not Emily Peterson."

Alex made a note of this, but I went on, telling him about Jerry-the-mechanic, and the way Melvin had apparently threatened his job, and the rivalry between Pete's father and Melvin.

Alex made thorough notes. "They are both on my list to interview today."

I also told him the details about the saffron grinder that was usually kept on the dining room table, but had been missing all week, and that Victoria suspected Rhonda of having it.

"Then there's the grease or dirt on my sliding glass door." Mallory pointed. "If the lab can confirm it is indeed grease, that would lead me to think that maybe Cindra was in my house."

I hated to admit it, but that sounded better to me than the idea of a stranger or someone with a deadly anger breaking into Mallory's house.

Alex twisted his lips and continued writing, but I got the sense he felt relief from this, too.

"I tried to ask Cindra about her family's spice grinders when we were alone in the lunchroom," Mallory said. We hadn't discussed this yet, so my gaze stayed trained on her, wondering what she discovered. But she added, "She changed the subject on me, and started in on all the people at the party who had hated her grandfather. I never did get her back around to the spice grinder."

"So you think Cindra was trying to point blame at someone else to cover her own tracks?" I asked.

"Or is she truly on the lookout for her grandfather's killer?" Alex suggested. "And she planted the spice grinder to tip us off of where to look?"

"The spice grinder showed up before the murder, though, so if she had wanted to catch the killer, wouldn't she have also been able to stop the murder?" Before I could answer, Mallory went on. "Besides, wouldn't the spice grinder have naturally led us to looking at Victoria?" This was true, and I didn't get the sense that Cindra believed anything bad of their chef.

"Or Mr. Peterson," I suggested. "Who always used the saffron at the table."

"Or the housekeeper, who Victoria believes last had the grinder in order to fill it." After making one final note, Alex flipped his yellow legal pad to the side to reveal an eight-by-ten photo of a water pump. It had a small, jagged puncture right in the center of the plastic housing, which had enough scuff marks, it appeared it may have been sawed into.

"Could that be wear and tear, from something rubbing against it?" Mallory asked.

Alex shook his head. "There were no other mechanisms nearby to wear against it. Forensics is convinced that by the roughness of this cut in the pump, it was a purposeful act. But even more importantly, right now they are trying to match up this cut with the metal blade they found jammed into the ground fault interrupter." He moved the photo aside to reveal a blackened outlet on the wall. "From my understanding, the pump would have sat unaffected until it was turned on by using the button that started the jets. Then it would have let water in through this gap." He pointed to the sawed-open hole in the pump. "Which should have tripped the ground fault interrupter, if this metal blade hadn't been inserted to prevent it from tripping."

"So someone knew what they were doing?" Mallory confirmed.

I hated to admit it, but the first name that came to mind was Cindra Peterson. Apparently, I wasn't alone.

"I'd be willing to bet Cindra knows all about tripping ground wires," Mallory said, her face serious.

I tilted my head at the photos. The one with the pump was close enough that I could see the jagged edges around the hole on the plastic casing. The outlet cover, while blackened, didn't have any other obvious signs of tampering. My green sea glass sat cool around my neck, as it had since I'd left Crystal Cove, and yet I had a warmth come over me that felt exactly like that same kind of intuition.

"You said it was a small blade that was jammed into there?" I pointed at the blackened outlet cover."

"Tiny." Alex flipped to the next photo, which had the outlet cover removed. Several of the wires behind the cover were also blackened. I pulled the photo closer, revealing the photo underneath, which I was guessing was the small blade that had been used both to puncture a hole into the pump and to prevent the electrical outlet from tripping.

I only glanced at that photo for a second, but Mallory reached for it and pulled it almost up to her face. "Do you still have this blade in evidence?" she asked Alex. "And what about the spice grinder?"

His brow furrowed. "They're both either still at the lab or logged in as evidence. Why?"

Mallory stood like she was ready to go there right this second. "Because the spice grinder we found under the Christmas tree was missing its blade, and if I had to guess, I'd say this blade is a match."

Chapter Twenty - Mallory

ALEX AND TABBY WANTED to finish their chess pie but I was in too much of a hurry to get to the lab. I quickly packed up the remainder of the pie, saying, "Let's eat the rest after we visit the lab."

If the blade was a match, what did that mean? At the very least, it meant that the spice grinder was placed under my Christmas tree for a very specific reason, as it was connected to the murder weapon.

I had been to the lab a couple of times before, always with Alex, but if any of the scientists recognized me, they didn't show it. The lab was a long narrow room with a white counter down the center. There were four scientists working at the moment, and while two of them said hello to Alex, no one looked at me or Tabby.

We arrived beside Scotty, and Alex asked, "Is Amber still in?"

Scotty pushed up his glasses as he looked from where he was studying something under a large microscope to Alex. "I sent her on an errand. She should be back any time." As usual, Scotty's words were all business. I wondered who had started calling this stoic man by such a casual nickname. I would have thought him to be much more of a "Scott."

Alex pulled a photo from his file and showed it to Scotty. "We're looking for the spice grinder I turned in. We think it may have significance in the Peterson case."

Scotty turned to a nearby laptop and started typing. Thirty seconds later, he said, "That was already logged with the property officer. It didn't contain any recognizable prints."

Alex nodded. "We think it could be a match for the blade that was found in the socket."

Scotty's eyebrows shot up. Clearly, they had not considered this possibility. "Let me put in a request to retrieve it. Do you have time to go pick it up?"

Alex nodded. "I'll make time."

I had no idea if the evidence lockup was on the premises or if Alex had to drive somewhere to get the item, but Scotty looked unimpressed when Alex said, "Wait here. I won't be long."

As soon as he left, I looked around the oblong room for somewhere we could stand that would be out of the way, but there was really nowhere. At the same time, I didn't want to have to make Tabby wait with me out in the chilly weather.

Scotty continued to stare at me, like he expected me to do something, though, and so I turned for the exit. I was about to take a step toward it when another thought occurred to me. "Have you heard anything back on the prints you took from my house yet?" Even though I know it wasn't my business to ask forensics directly for this information, I couldn't help myself, and added, "We're looking specifically for the substance that was found on the latch of the sliding door."

Scotty, unfortunately, only continued to stare at me. He knew I helped Alex from time to time, but I had never been in here asking questions on my own.

I wracked my brain, searching for the right words that would make him trust me with this information. Tabby spoke up before I came up with any.

"You see, one of our suspects works at Big Rig Machinery. If we could confirm the substance to be grease, specifically a grease that would be used on large machinery, this could tell us something that would be helpful for the case."

Honesty. That was Tabby's choice in how to dig up our own intel, and as

I continued to watch Scotty, I saw the second he made a decision. It worked. I was impressed with Tabby's ability to size up the situation and know the right angle instinctively.

Scotty turned back for his laptop and typed again, for several long minutes, and I suppressed the urge to move in and try to read over his shoulder. Finally, he turned back to us. "We've done presumptive testing, and I can tell you it is indeed an industrial grease product. Whether or not it matches the specific grease found at Big Rig Machinery, I can't confirm that."

We both nodded. That was still helpful. I couldn't think of a single reason why Alex, Amber, Tabby, or I would have touched a greasy hand on that latch anytime in the last several months.

"Could you tell the age of the grease?" I asked.

He resumed typing for several more minutes. "From our preliminary report, the grease does not appear to be degraded." He looked at me over his shoulder and explained in layman's terms. "It was likely fresh."

I stepped back against the wall to give Scotty as much room as possible to proceed with his work, and Tabby followed suit. "All this leads me to think Cindra was in my house," I told her in a quiet murmur.

She nodded. "Me too. Now it's just a matter of why she was in there. If Cindra killed her grandfather, would there be any reason for her to plant a spice grinder under your Christmas tree ahead of time?"

I took a big breath as I thought that over. "None that I can think of."

Before we had time to discuss it any further, Alex returned with a baggie. Inside, I could see the steel and wood-grain spice grinder. Scotty took it from Alex and called out, "Hal, are you still working on that blade from case 829?"

A man in a white lab coat several feet away said, "Haven't had time yet, but I have it here." Scotty must have been the man's superior, because he left the computer he was working at to immediately bring the blade over. It was also packed in a plastic baggie with a typewritten sticker on the outside. The only words I could make out on the sticker before Scotty was opening the baggie were "hot tub" and "unknown" and "Peterson."

Before Scotty reached into the bag, he slid on a pair of blue latex gloves and switched on the headlamp that rested on his forehead. He took off his regular glasses and slipped on a pair that looked much thicker. Then he reached in and pulled out the blade.

It was tiny, no more than an inch long and half the width of my pinkie. It appeared to be stainless steel with either end bent up. One end was blackened, and I had to guess that one had been in the wall socket. The other end appeared like it had been used to try to carve into cement. Or perhaps to puncture a hole into a hot tub pump.

Scotty held it carefully between two gloved fingers while Alex donned his own gloves and I pointed to show him where to turn the spice grinder to open it up to where the blade should go. He turned it, pulled off the end and then held it open for Scotty.

Scotty pressed the blade into the spice grinder, and it was a perfect fit.

Chapter Twenty-one - Tabby

WE HAD THE MURDER weapon. We had a good idea of the intruder into Mallory's house. What we didn't know was if the murderer and intruder were the same person. We also didn't know the motive for any of it.

Alex thanked Scotty and asked him to look closer at the blade and the spice grinder as soon as he had a moment. We headed out into the hallway that led to the police station. As soon as we got out there, Amber arrived back from her errand, which apparently was getting coffee for some of the other scientists. She carried a compostable tray with four coffee cups. Since there were four scientists working at the moment, I guessed none of them were for her, and made a mental note to make her a special drink as soon as she was next at Mallory's house.

"They sent you out for coffee in this weather?" Alex asked. I liked how protective he seemed over Amber.

She rolled her eyes. "Kirk is working today. He has to prove his dominance over someone around here."

I didn't know who Kirk was, but I was glad we hadn't had to ask him for any favors.

"I'll talk to him," Alex said, but Amber groaned and said, "Please don't. This is my job. Trust me to do it, okay?"

Alex smiled and nodded. "You're right. Okay. But the guy won't be getting a Christmas gift from me next year, I'll tell you that much."

Amber smiled at this, but only for half a second. Then she got down to business. "Why are you all down here? Did you figure something out?"

Alex quickly explained to her the match between the blade and the spice grinder, and then Mallory added the bit we'd found out about the grease on her sliding door latch.

Amber's eyes widened. "So Cindra broke into your house?"

Mallory pressed her hands toward the floor. "We don't know that for sure. I mean, how would she even know where I lived, and why would she think I would investigate something like that?"

"Well..." Amber looked down, as though the answer embarrassed her. "I guess I kind of bragged a bit to Cindra. I was trying to show my worth to her, you know. I mean, a while ago. Back when we went to school together."

Amber let out another groan, clearly frustrated with herself for not explaining this well. "I don't really know Cindra. I mean, it was a few years ago when we went to school together, before I started online schooling. I'd taken a class in welding, mostly because my mom wanted me only in academic classes. It was my way of rebelling, and well, whatever. You don't care about that. Anyway, I had the definite sense that Cindra didn't appreciate me taking up space in her classroom. She seemed nice enough to me last night, though."

I would not have described Cindra's interactions last night as "nice," but that seemed unimportant at the moment.

"Anyway, because she was such a natural with welding and I wasn't, I told her how you and I solved my dad's murder together," she said to Mallory, "and how you used to be married to a mystery writer and had been teaching me all about solving crimes. At the time I was so proud of what we'd done, I thought it might impress her, but she barely reacted, like I didn't even know if she had heard me."

That seemed pretty much how Cindra reacted to everything, in my opinion.

"So you told her my name?" Mallory asked.

Amber shrugged. "Probably."

"So it would have been easy for her to figure out where Mallory lived?" Alex clarified.

Amber bit her lip, looking down and nodding.

"That's all good information," I said, wanting to make Amber feel better. It wasn't her fault, after all, that she'd told someone about her investigative success over two years ago. "Now can we think of any reason why anyone else from the Peterson household or anyone at their Christmas party would know where you live?" I asked Mallory. "Did you meet with Emily Peterson prior to the party? Did she come to your house?"

Mallory shook her head. "We spoke twice on the phone. She e-transferred me the deposit."

I nodded slowly. "And how did she hear about your catering services?"

Mallory looked to Amber. "I have no idea. I assumed maybe word of mouth? I had an ad in the paper back in October before you got so busy with school."

"We weren't catering back when I spoke to Cindra in school, so I doubt she knew," Amber said.

"Martinez?" A deep voice echoed from the end of the hallway. The man was short and on the plump side with a bushy gray mustache and an angry scowl. "I've been looking everywhere for you!"

"Sorry, Captain," Alex said. "I was just on my way back to my desk."

The police captain's gaze was not on Alex. It was directed squarely at Mallory, and she seemed to cower under it.

"We were just leaving," Mallory said. "Come on, Tabby."

Amber didn't even say goodbye to any of us. She pushed through the door into the lab, clearly wanting to get away as soon as possible from this police captain I'd heard so much about.

And I had to admit, as Mallory led me in the opposite direction to the nearest exit, I was in no hurry to be the next person on the captain's bad side.

Chapter Twenty-two – Mallory

ALL THE WAY HOME and even once we were in the house, Tabby and I kept discussing the details of the case over and over again, looking for what we had missed. While Hunch hadn't been allowed to accompany us into the forensics lab, he paced around the house within inches of my feet now, unwilling to miss a single word that was said about the case.

"Is there any reason at all that Cindra would have planted the spice grinder for us to find if she was the person to kill her grandfather?" Tabby asked, following me as I made my way into the kitchen to clean up after my tornado that had culminated in a Chess Pie.

I'd been thinking about this nonstop, too. "An ego thing? Because she wanted to be found out? Or because she wanted to plant suspicion toward Victoria?"

"Could that be why she was so helpful in setting up a meeting with Victoria at her work? Or could she have been planting suspicion toward her dad? He was the one who liked saffron, after all, and we don't really know how she feels about him."

"Or..." I said, "could Conrad Peterson have actually killed his own father? Remember that he was fairly ambivalent about it only moments after the old man was discovered dead."

"You're right!" Tabby sounded excited by this prospect. Even though we barely knew Cindra, we both seemed to be looking for any answer that didn't make her a mean-hearted killer. Our bias was likely only due to her age, but I felt a clear sense of relief at having another suspect to focus on.

I immediately texted Alex our thoughts, but less than five minutes later, I had a response that deflated my hopes.

Alex: Forensics narrowed the puncturing of the pump to less than an hour prior to the electrocution. Otherwise, it would have been completely full of water which it was not. I understand from Conrad Peterson that he only arrived home from a flight right before the party at around six p.m. That doesn't seem

like it would have given him time to do this but I will confirm his flight details with the airline to make certain of this before removing him completely from suspicion.

I read the text aloud to Tabby.

"He had just come in from outside," she said. "Do you remember? When he first came in and helped himself to your warm appetizers, he had snow in his hair? And there was a suitcase in the mudroom when we left, but not when we arrived."

I did remember that. "If the spice grinder was there to point suspicion at Conrad Peterson, it won't work if he has a clear alibi. If it was used to point suspicion toward Victoria, the only person I know of who seems to dislike Victoria is Emily Peterson."

"And she also hated Melvin," Tabby put in.

I stopped loading the dishwasher and tapped a finger to my mouth. "I just don't see her as capable of rigging a hot tub. Teach a yoga class? Probably. But not electrical wiring."

Chapter Twenty-three - Tabby

FOR THE REST OF the afternoon, Mallory and I talked through the case and I made detailed notes in my spreadsheet.

Conrad Peterson had possible motive, even if it was compassionate, and perhaps the means to do it, but we had already heard back from Alex that his flight details were confirmed, so he did not have opportunity.

I grudgingly crossed him off my suspect list and then tapped my finger over Emily Peterson's name.

She had motive and opportunity, but did she have the means? We had suggested her as a suspect to Alex as well, but he'd said that during his interview with her, she'd made a point of telling him she knew nothing at all about electrical wiring and kept turning that conversation back to Cindra.

I looked up from the kitchen table to where Mallory was cooking something again, even though I was stuffed. Thanks to the questions that had arisen in this case, she'd been feeding me all day. "Do you get the feeling she was overplaying her ignorance?"

Mallory paused her kneading and turned to me. "Back when my husband was alive, he took care of all the house repairs and such. I usually just asked him for help when I blew a fuse or had any other electrical problem." Her face flushed like she was embarrassed by her ignorance. I had a father who had taught me and my siblings how to do everything from change car tires to putty holes in walls. I guess I'd just assumed everyone knew the basics of how to fix things around a house. Then again, I wouldn't have known how to rig a hot tub to electrocute someone without first electrocuting myself.

I nibbled my lip, looking for the holes. "I guess we don't even know exactly how long she's lived there."

"Three years," Mallory told me, getting back to her dough. "Cindra mentioned it while we were in the machinery lunchroom."

Three years may have been long enough for the average person to know a bit about the electrical wiring in their house, but perhaps not a woman who had servants for such things. That seemed like a dead end so I moved on.

There was Victoria. Again, she had opportunity, probably more than anyone in the house. But did she have the means? She also didn't strike me as someone who knew how to fiddle with electrical wiring, not to mention the hot tub pump. And she, more than anyone, lacked motive.

But then I looked over my notes again and remembered she may have been in line for some money from the old man, and she had a desperate need for money.

"Did you talk to the brother at all? Benedict? Tall thin guy in a blue dress shirt?" I asked, making a note of his name.

Mallory squinted, like she didn't remember him, but then she said, "I could have sworn he was wearing a white shirt."

Hmm. Now that she mentioned it, I thought I remembered that, too. "If he changed shirts, does that mean he lives there?"

"He certainly kept an eye on the place as if he does," Mallory said. But neither of us had much else to add beneath his name, as he had kept to himself most of the evening, as much as we had seen.

I added Rhonda the housekeeper next. She may have been angry with both Melvin and Victoria because Victoria had been given the night off but not her. She also would most likely have been the person to take the spice grinder to refill it. She could have easily gone upstairs during the party without being noticed.

There was the hot tub mechanic, who had been forced to work during his vacation and had his profession threatened. He definitely had means and opportunity, but was that enough motive to want to kill the old man?

But then why invite him to the Christmas party? Perhaps to make up for something he said?

The redhead named Pete was the second last on my list. All I really knew about this man was that he had a gorgeous wife, one who seemed a bit out of his league, his father had been a rival of Melvin's, and he'd been irritated by Melvin not showing up to his own party. Not a very strong motive, and was there any reason to think he had means or opportunity? Then again, was there any reason to think he didn't?

And finally, reluctantly, I filled in the row for Cindra Peterson. She clearly had the means, and she'd been upstairs around the time of Melvin's death, so she had opportunity. Her motive may have been one of compassion, but it was still motive.

I started to read my notes out loud to Mallory. Her kneading intensified a little as she said, "Let's go back to the mechanic." It seemed she was as frustrated by this case as I was.

When I read off the small bit of information I had on Jerry the mechanic, she stopped and turned to me, holding up her flour-covered fingers. "But, wait. Jerry worked on the hot tub on the

22nd, right? And Alex said the pump was tampered with less than an hour prior to Melvin Peterson's electrocution?"

"You're right." I nodded as I typed this into my phone.

"Could Jerry have gone upstairs during the party without anyone noticing?"

"The stairs were in plain view. He could certainly have headed up there, but someone would have seen him." I marked this down as another question we could ask other party-goers. But then I remembered something. "You know, it was just before dinner that I overheard that group with Jerry and Pete talking. Each of them were trying to convince the other to go up and tell Melvin to get over his offense and come down to his own party. Both of them laughed and said there was no way they were going to do that." I made notes as I remembered this.

"So we're back to Cindra being our prime suspect?" Mallory thumped her dough onto the counter. That was the part of this investigation that was upsetting her. In truth, I wanted to find a reason not to blame the girl as much as she did.

And as I thought that, I came up with an idea. Alex had tried to arrange another interview with the Petersons, but had been put off until tomorrow. He had been frustrated by this, and Mallory had mentioned how thankful he was for her help whenever he was facing obstacles in a case.

"Hey, Mallory?" When she looked over her shoulder, agitation clear on her face, I said, "Didn't we forget something over at the Petersons? Your good chef's knife, or something." The more the idea formed, the more I felt a strong need to get over there tonight, right now. My heart thumped faster and I had the feeling someone was going to end up in danger if we didn't.

Mallory shook her head, not catching on. "I already put my knives away, they're right…" She trailed off as she motioned to her wrapped knives on the back of the counter. Suddenly, she seemed to get where I was going with this. "Right. Maybe we should get back over there tonight and look for it?"

I loved how easily Mallory trusted my intuition, and how even I was starting to trust my intuition more myself. I nodded, a smile forming. "Yes, we definitely should."

Chapter Twenty-four - Mallory

WE ARRIVED AT THE Peterson's house just after six. I'd had a quick conversation with Alex about it. He had confirmed with Jerry that he had fixed the hot tub on the 22nd and had not been in the solarium since that time. Alex was stuck waiting for Cindra outside Big Rig Machinery before his next interview with Pete, and quickly gave us the okay to go over to the Petersons under the guise of looking for a kitchen tool.

Tabby and I had been talking about the family for the entire drive over—Emily,

Conrad, and Cindra—but the instant I set eyes on the housekeeper, Rhonda, I tried to focus on what notes Tabby had made about her. Her meticulously ironed black clothes and white apron, along with her tight dark bun, told me she was all business, and I remembered that about her. She had desperately wanted to follow her employer's orders and keep everything about Melvin's death quiet.

Thankfully, Tabby hadn't spent the last hour baking a buttery braided brioche, and instead had her head in the game.

"It's Rhonda, isn't it?" Tabby said, stretching out a hand. As usual, Hunch had not wanted me to leave him behind, and on this one occasion, I figured we needed his help so I blocked Rhonda's view of the doorway and at the same time made a big motion of taking off my coat and passing it to the housekeeper to distract her as Hunch snuck by her feet.

Rhonda clearly was used to doing what she was told without a second thought. After automatically taking my coat, she stared down at it for several long seconds.

"Can we come in for a minute?" Tabby practically pushed her way inside the front entryway, not about to be told no. She peaked around the corner before taking time to remove her boots. "Are Mr. and Mrs. Peterson home?"

Rhonda finally had her wits about her, racing over to block Tabby's slushy booted entry to the rest of the house. "They should be home any minute. Are they expecting you?"

I had already removed my boots, so I took over from here. "We seem to be missing a very specific peeler of ours, and we thought we may have left it here. Mrs. Peterson hasn't been picking up her phone, so I thought I'd just drop by and check."

I'd called both Emily Peterson and Cindra before coming over. I'd left a message for Cindra, but at the last second I figured we may get more truthful information from Emily with a sneak attack.

By this time, Tabby had gotten out of her boots, which seemed to calm Rhonda somewhat. "While we're here, can I ask you about a spice grinder you may have?"

Right! The spice grinder. That was at least one thing we had to ask Rhonda about.

Rhonda pulled back. "I could get Victoria. She knows more about the kitchen supplies than I do."

"Sure." Tabby led the way toward the kitchen and Rhonda looked torn between following her and going upstairs to grab Victoria. "I'll ask her before I go," Tabby added, when Rhonda made the decision to follow her. I trailed behind.

Tabby headed straight for the cupboard that held the full set of spice grinders.

"We were admiring your spices last night during the party. Those grinders aren't cheap."

Rhonda shrugged, like she hadn't noticed one way or the other. "The Petersons believe in buying quality items. Like I said, if you want to know more about them, you should probably ask the house chef, Victoria."

I didn't notice any animosity in Rhonda when she spoke of Victoria.

Tabby pulled out the pepper grinder. "I've seen plenty of pretty pepper grinders like this one over the years, but I've never seen the tiny ones like the saffron one you had on your dining room table. Do you know where I could get a small one like that?"

I watched Rhonda carefully, but not a hint of surprise flickered on her face. Only exasperation. "Like I said, I have no idea about the kitchen supplies. I'll go get Victoria."

"Wait." I stepped into her path. I wanted to keep her on her own for just one more minute. She looked annoyed, but she didn't fight me. "As the housekeeper, aren't you the one who fills the spices?" I hoped I didn't sound ridiculously out of left field with this question, but I had to know while we still had her on her own.

She gave me a strange look, but at least she answered. "Well, I add them to my shopping list when Victoria says we need something. I don't actually refill them. In fact, I have no idea how to open those things."

I studied her to see if she was lying. She didn't appear to be. Still, I pushed. "Oh, I understood you actually stepped in to help as their cook for the house for a while?"

Her eyes narrowed. "Who told you that?"

I shrugged, trying to bring this back to a casual conversation and ease her into talking more. "I can't remember who mentioned it. Cindra? Or maybe Emily? Anyway, I just assumed if you had worked in the kitchen, you'd know all about the spice grinders and how to refill them. I have to refill some of mine, like my oregano one, every other month." I let out what I hoped was a lighthearted chuckle.

It seemed to work. Rhonda gave a small shrug and a sheepish smile edged onto her face. "I did cook for a while, but I was never any good at it, and the whole family let me know that often. Thankfully, Marissa and Benny used to take over the kitchen regularly back then, and I could always count on them to fix anything that was broken or fill the spices if they needed refilling."

Cindra had mentioned a Marissa, so this lined up, but who was Benny? It also made me think that if Rhonda found refilling a spice grinder too difficult, she definitely would not have been able to rig the electrical wiring of the hot tub.

Before I could launch into my next question, Rhonda said, "If you're going to be looking through kitchen cupboards for your peeler, I should get Victoria down here regardless." She pushed past me.

As soon as she left the room, Tabby whispered, "I'm going to check the dining room for the saffron grinder—just in case."

I nodded and while she was gone, I double-checked the rest of the spice cupboard, to make sure it wasn't here. I was fairly convinced we wouldn't find it, since the exact same spice grinder had been in the lab this afternoon, but Tabby was smart, making sure we weren't following some sort of loose thread that wouldn't lead anywhere.

Tabby returned only seconds later wearing a perplexed look and holding a small white slip of paper. "Look. I think it's the same as the one we found in the saffron grinder."

I moved close beside her as she placed it flat onto the island so we could both read it.

NOT WHERE IT BELONGED BUT WAS THERE NONETHELESS.

"It was at the back of the hutch in the dining room, covered by a Christmas garland," she said.

I had snapped a photo of the note we'd found in the saffron grinder before we'd gone out shopping on the morning of the 26th to look for more clues, so I pulled it up on my phone.

THE TOWEL CLOSET ISN'T WHERE THIS BELONGS. TIME TO INVESTIGATE!

"Is this new note still referring to the saffron grinder?" I asked. "Should we be looking in all the house's towel closets?"

Before Tabby could answer Rhonda walked back into the kitchen. Victoria followed close behind her. As before, her eyes were rimmed with red. Both ladies looked down at the swatch of typewritten paper on the island, but neither took time to so much as ask what it was. It seemed there was no recognition in either of them, so I seamlessly slid it into my pocket as I asked, "You didn't happen to see my vegetable peeler around here anywhere?" to Victoria.

"You didn't say you were missing anything when I talked to you earlier," Victoria said in way of a hello. She was still in her sweater and jeans we'd seen her in earlier. I wondered if she wore the same type of monochrome outfit as Rhonda when she was working. Tabby had told me about the final question she'd hit her with while leaving Big Rig Machinery earlier today and the way she had raced away, not wanting to answer.

She'd asked if Emily Peterson hated Melvin enough to want him dead.

"We didn't notice until I went to use the peeler this afternoon. I was hoping to add chocolate shavings to my brioche." This wasn't true, but it sounded like a good excuse. "Is Cindra home by any chance?"

"No," Rhonda answered. "She's been working late these days."

"What did your peeler look like?" Victoria strode for the kitchen island and pulled out a drawer that held dozens of kitchen utensils, clearly wanting to keep us on task.

"It was tiny, all silver," I said, joining her by the drawer. In truth, the peeler I used for chocolate had a bright green handle, but since we weren't actually looking for it, I went with something that would supposedly take me longer to find in this mishmash of utensils. "Tabby, why don't you ask her about that grinder you were interested in while I look." I kept my peripheral vision trained on Victoria as I continued my ruse of searching through the drawer.

Victoria didn't make any sudden movements, but that was all I could tell for sure.

"Oh yeah. You told me earlier that Mr. Peterson liked to grind saffron onto almost everything. I was interested to see a tiny grinder like these ones..." Tabby motioned to the pepper grinder, "that a person might use for saffron."

"Well, like I said, that one is being refilled. You must have it, right?" Victoria asked Rhonda as she strode across the kitchen.

I looked up from the drawer to see Rhonda shaking her head. "I had so much to worry about with supplies for the party, I didn't get to the specialty store yet to get the saffron. It's still on my list."

Victoria didn't seem to notice that she hadn't mentioned the grinder itself. She dug through the cupboard behind the biggest spice grinders in the front to find the celery seed. "But we have at least one more small one like it. See?" She passed it over to Tabby.

Tabby immediately took off the cap, looking like she had a general admiration for the thing, but even from across the kitchen I could tell she was looking for the blade, which appeared to be where it should be in this grinder.

My phone buzzed in my pocket. I pulled it out to see a text from Alex.

Alex: I've been waiting outside Big Rig Machinery for an hour. When the last guy locked up I asked if Cindra was

still in there. He said she left claiming she had cramps a couple of hours ago. Is she at the house? Does it seem like she has cramps? Let me know when you're done and I'll head over there to interview her.

I replied with a quick: **She's not here.** I'd have to elaborate later, but I had to admit, it seemed suspicious to me that she'd apparently been working late but when the police were looking for her, she happened to have left early. I quickly added, **We're almost done here. If you have time to meet at my place I have some new info.**

Victoria pulled out another tiny grinder, which I knew to contain anise, and passed it over for Tabby to make the same observations. "Oh, and here's one more."

"Do you have any idea where these were purchased?" Tabby asked, casually.

Victoria looked to Rhonda. "That was before my time, I'm afraid. Do you have any idea?"

Rhonda shook her head. "I already told them I couldn't help." Then to us, "You'll want to call Mrs. Peterson and ask her if you have any other questions about them."

I was getting the sense that it was simply Rhonda's personality to be all-business about her job. I didn't get the idea she was hiding anything, and I also didn't get the sense there was any animosity between the chef and the housekeeper.

Even without Amber's forensic training, Alex's detective training, or Tabby's intuition, I had enough experience to recognize that neither of these two were guilty. I had been struggling a little lately to figure out my place now that Alex and Amber were spending so much time together, but this case was reassuring me that I still had something to contribute.

It was clear to me that neither Victoria nor Rhonda had broken into my house or killed Melvin Peterson, and they likely had not framed anyone for doing it either.

Chapter Twenty-five - Tabby

"ONE MORE THING," MALLORY said as we
followed Rhonda and Victoria through
the living room toward the entrance.
She'd finally admitted the peeler she was
looking for wasn't here after stalling and
searching every drawer in the kitchen.
"You haven't by chance noticed anything
unusual in any of the towel cupboards?"
She followed this up with a lighthearted
chuckle. Mallory always impressed me
at how she could lighten up the tone of
an otherwise serious interview. She was
naturally such a nurturer—everywhere
from a kitchen to a crime scene—with

a warmth and humor that put people instantly at ease and added a human touch to these situations.

Both house employees looked bewildered by the question. Victoria stopped at the stairs and said, "I hope you find your peeler." Apparently neither of them felt compelled to answer Mallory's nonsensical question, and unfortunately I couldn't think of any way to help make sense of it for them. Without another word, Victoria headed up the stairs.

Mallory and I stopped in place looking at each other. I could tell she was as eager as I was to search out this second clue before we left. Rhonda turned when she realized we weren't following. She cleared her throat, as though that might move along our exit.

I glanced up to see that Victoria had disappeared upstairs. Then I turned back to Rhonda. "Victoria seemed concerned about her job, now that Melvin Peterson has passed. Are you feeling concerned about yours?"

Rhonda let out a humorless laugh. "If Victoria's concerned about her job, it's not because of the old man's death."

"No?" Mallory and I both asked at once.

Rhonda seemed surprised by our interest, but at least she answered. "Just last week, I overheard Mr. Peterson arguing with his dad over his wife, Emily. The old man told him if he didn't get rid of that wife of his, he'd do it for him. I heard the whole thing, but neither of them knew I was there. Victoria's young. She's not as talented about being discreet. She walked right in on them, and they suddenly stopped talking. I stayed out of sight and heard Conrad Peterson threaten her, telling her if she knows what's good for her, she'd keep her mouth shut about anything she heard."

Mallory and I both had wide eyes and Rhonda seemed to like that she'd surprised us with her little bit of gossip. We'd found an area that she didn't feel compelled to keep her business-like sense. She lowered her voice and went on to say, "To tell you the truth, I don't think Victoria even heard any of the conversation. But regardless, everyone knows she would have been on Melvin's side. It just doesn't put her in a great position now that he's gone."

"Wow." Mallory shook her head. "You said Conrad threatened Victoria. Do you think he would actually do something to hurt her?"

"Oh, no!" Rhonda seemed taken aback at the suggestion. "I only meant he'd threatened her job. Mr. Peterson doesn't have it in him to physically hurt anyone." By her tone, I suspected Rhonda sided more with the junior Mr. Peterson. She likely felt as though he was the one with the power to hire and fire, but I thought again about Cindra's words over lunch—she had thought all the staff would be replaced within the month.

I was glad to hear Rhonda's response, though, even if we had pretty much already cleared Mr. Peterson from our suspect list because of his alibi. Still, I wouldn't want to think that Victoria could be in danger for working here.

Then again, this new information certainly gave Emily Peterson a stronger motive to kill Melvin.

I didn't know what else to ask until my eyes caught on the Christmas tree, which stood unlit today. "That's lovely silver gift wrap. Where did you get it?" I walked toward it, because it looked to be the same patterned wrap that we'd found the spice grinder wrapped in underneath Mallory's tree.

I bypassed the gold foil-wrapped gifts and picked up a very light-feeling silver box as Rhonda waved a hand and said, "Those are just for decoration. There's nothing in them."

Mallory followed me over. "Yes, but Tabby's right. This gift wrap is lovely." We both stared at Rhonda, waiting for an answer.

Finally, she said, "I'm sure Mrs. Peterson picked it up somewhere. I couldn't tell you."

Again, this came back to Emily Peterson. I didn't know what else to ask, and clearly Mallory didn't either, because she hesitantly started to walk toward the entry, saying, "We'd better get back to my place to meet Alex."

But we hadn't made it out of the living room when suddenly a ruckus sounded from the door, and then Emily and Conrad's voices, as they were in mid-argument.

"All I'm saying is that you could have just gone with cremation," Emily said. "He's not going to know the difference now."

"And you wouldn't care if your last wishes weren't observed?" Conrad stopped speaking when he entered the living room and saw they weren't alone.

"Hi!" Mallory said, too brightly. "I thought I left my vegetable peeler here, but I couldn't find it anywhere."

Emily and Conrad Peterson looked at each other for a long moment before turning back to Mallory.

"You're only here as my caterer, then?" Emily's eyes narrowed and I wondered what other capacity she possibly thought we were here under. She quickly cleared that up. "One of the forensics team mentioned that it was fortunate we had some caterers on hand who regularly helped Detective Martinez investigate. But you certainly wouldn't have shown up under false pretenses today, would you?" Her narrowed eyes came with a side of raised eyebrows.

I glanced at Rhonda, whose face paled at this realization of who we were. Mallory's face reddened, and I suspected mine had as well. But she sounded just as cool as ever when she replied. "I've had the peeler since culinary school. It's really important to me." Her words sounded so genuine, even I believed that she'd had the peeler that long, and, in fact, I almost even believed the thing was missing, even though I'd seen it with my own eyes this morning. "But while I have you here, would you mind at all if I asked you a couple of questions?" She sounded very sweet and unassuming.

"I don't know about Emily," Conrad said. "But I have to grab my suitcase and catch a flight." He didn't wait for any kind of argument and headed for the stairs. Hadn't Alex been planning to meet with him again tomorrow morning?

Even though we had pretty much cleared him from suspicion, his avoidance of the police didn't look good. Besides, it could have been helpful to have him here as we questioned Emily. Then again, I had a feeling it may be easier to catch her in a lie all on her own, without her husband here.

"I don't have long, either," Emily told us with a huff. "Rhonda, will you tell Cindra we have to leave in ten minutes for the book signing? And be sure to tell her to dress respectfully if she wants my help to meet the author."

I opened my mouth to confirm that Emily and Cindra were truly going to a book signing together, but before I could say anything, Rhonda answered.

"I'm afraid Cindra isn't home yet, Mrs. Peterson."

Emily's forehead buckled. She turned to her housekeeper. "She hasn't come home from work? She's been begging me for months to introduce her to Gregory Roland and now she hasn't even shown up? I don't believe it."

Rhonda checked her watch. "She still has ten minutes."

Emily balked. "If she hasn't been home since work, what do you think she's going to look like? I am not taking her to the signing in her greasy grubby clothes."

"I—" Rhonda blocked Mallory with her back as she told Emily, "I'm just going to go and call her cell phone and see where she's at. I'll bet she's on her way. I'm sure she didn't forget."

Emily sighed. "I really can't imagine that." She sighed again and dismissed her

housekeeper with, "Thank you, Rhonda."
Emily turned back to Mallory once
Rhonda was out of the room. "Now
I already answered about a hundred
questions for your detective boss.
You know you should really introduce
yourself as a police assistant when
you're hired as a caterer."

Mallory tilted her head and asked the
obvious question. "Oh? Why's that?"

Emily Peterson huffed and took off her
coat to distract from the question. She
laid it over the back of the couch,
apparently for Rhonda to deal with later,
and headed for the kitchen. "Whatever it
is, I sure hope you don't plan to take long
with it. Let's see if I can find that peeler
while you ask whatever it is you came
here for, and then you can be on your
way." She sounded beyond irritated, but

Mallory followed her into the kitchen, unbothered. I trailed behind.

Mallory pulled a pad of paper and a pen from her purse, which suddenly made her look very official. "Now I understand Melvin Peterson was the owner of this house and you and he didn't get—"

Emily wasn't about to let Mallory finish that sentence. She waved an annoyed hand. "Oh, come on. Our family got on just fine! How would you like people poking into your family's troubles in the midst of your grief?" With her question, suddenly she had tears streaming down her face. She grabbed for three tissues from a box on the island and made a show of wiping at them, but her face was still wet when she pulled them away.

"So you're saying you and Melvin Peterson got along well?" Mallory asked, undeterred. I studied Emily Peterson carefully as she grasped for an excuse.

"We had our arguments, same as any family." As she spoke, she avoided our eyes and yanked open drawers, pulling out much of the contents and plopping them on the island, under the guise of searching for our peeler. She left all the contents strewn about for someone else to clean up. "Now that cannot be what you've come to ask me about." She let out a cackle of a laugh to make this sound ridiculous, rather than the serious motive it was, to have had contention with a man who had just been murdered.

While she was busy, I pulled the fennel spice grinder from the cupboard. "We were looking for your saffron grinder. Any idea where it went?" I watched her carefully, but she only appeared confused at my question.

"Saffron is expensive. Why would I let you use my saffron grinder?"

Mallory interjected. "We don't want to use it, Mrs. Peterson. We would just like to see it. It may or may not be a part of our investigation."

Emily pulled back. "Part of what investigation? Melvin didn't even like saffron."

"Is that right?" Mallory focused on her notepad and jotted this down. "We would still like to see the spice grinder, if you don't mind." It sounded like it wouldn't make any difference if Emily did mind, and a second later, she huffed and spun toward the dining room.

Interesting. So she clearly thought it was still in there.

We followed her and watched as she searched the side hutch, pulling the Christmas garland onto the floor, and then every inch of the long table.
She shook her head. "Someone must have put it back in the cupboard." She sounded like this move was offensive. She marched back for the kitchen and then pulled all the spice grinders onto the counter as she said, "You'll have to at least tell me how you think a grinder filled with saffron might be important in any kind of investigation into that old man."

"I'm afraid that's police business," Mallory said.

When Emily got to the last of the spices, I had an idea and handed her the fennel.

"Do you know how to open this to refill it, Mrs. Peterson?"

She grabbed it from me, and with one twist it was open. Again, interesting. At least she wasn't playing ignorant where the spice grinders were concerned.

"I understand the saffron grinder was empty," Mallory said.

Emily nodded. "Oh that's right, it was. I'll bet Rhonda or Victoria put it somewhere to refill it. Now, really, if that's the end of your nonsensical questions..." She was about to head for the kitchen door again, when her husband walked through, wheeling a suitcase behind him.

"I'm off," he said. He went along the opposite side of the island from Emily. "Benny wants to talk to you when you're done. I told him you were with the caterers, talking about police business again."

Benny? As in Benedict?

Emily asked her husband, "Do you have any idea where to find that daughter of yours? She was supposed to go to that book signing with me with that author I went to school with and she's not even home."

Conrad turned and his forehead creased. "She hasn't come home from work yet?"

"Nope." Emily pursed her lips. "These ladies keep asking me about spices and vegetable peelers and treating me as if I'm doing something suspicious, but if anyone is suspicious, it's your daughter, you know that, right?"

Concern etched Conrad's face, but after a pause, apparently he wasn't going to defend anyone, even his own daughter. He turned and headed toward the mudroom, mumbling something that sounded like, "Fix this" as he passed his wife. He left without another word or so much as a kiss on the cheek.

As soon as he was out of the room, Emily turned back to us. "Have you questioned Cindra yet?" Before either of us could answer, she tsked and shook her head. "Poor child has not adjusted well to her father finding happiness." She tsked again as I tried to reconcile her statement.

Conrad Peterson did not seem like he'd found happiness with this woman, and perhaps Cindra had not adjusted well, but as far as I could tell from Amber, the girl seemed like the same kind of stoic, no-nonsense type of person she had been in high school.

"We spoke to Cindra, earlier today," Mallory told her. "And you are saying it's unusual for her not to be home at this time?"

"Very unusual." Emily gave an exaggerated nod and widened her eyes, as if to demonstrate her own innocence as she added, "I wonder what that girl could possibly be up to now. Is she also a suspect in your investigation? Because if she's hiding away to avoid the police, it definitely makes her look guilty of something, now doesn't it?"

While I didn't trust Emily Peterson's opinion of her stepdaughter, I had to admit, all signs of guilt did seem to point toward Cindra Peterson.

Chapter Twenty-six - Mallory

"Do you have a cell phone number for Cindra?" I asked, even though I already had Cindra's number. But I wanted to get a better sense from Emily if she had any idea where her stepdaughter could truly be, or if she was simply trying to divert my attention away from how vehemently she had hated the man who was now dead.

I had no idea if Alex had mentioned to her that the case had been escalated to homicide, but I suspected by the way she kept pointing us toward Cindra, she knew there had been foul play involved, either because she'd been told or because she'd been involved in the murder.

Emily sighed. "Yes, I have her number somewhere in my phone, but I don't bother using it because she never picks up for me. Do you want it?"

"Please," I said.

She pulled her own phone from a pocket and scrolled through. When she rattled off a number and I scribbled in into my notepad, I glanced over her shoulder and I could see she had Cindra listed as "Shrew" in her contacts.

When she saw me looking, she clicked her phone off and tucked it away in her pocket. "Why don't you have one more look for your peeler and I'll go check with

Rhonda, to see if she was able to get through to Cindra?"

She didn't wait for a response as she swept out of the room. We had no need to look through her mess of utensils out on the island, but this would at least give Tabby and me a chance to confer.

"What do you think?" Tabby asked. "Should we just let ourselves out while she's gone and go looking for Cindra?"

"Where?" I asked as I pulled open drawers and cupboards around the kitchen. "The only place I would know to look is at her job, and Alex says she's not there. He's going to meet us at our place, though, so maybe we should just head there and come up with a plan."

"What are you looking for?" Tabby asked.

"A towel cupboard. Oh, wait. Here they are." I pulled out stacks of kitchen towels and Tabby looked through them, shaking each one out. We had barely gotten through the stack with unfolded towels now covering most of the utensils on the island when Emily Peterson returned.

"You're still here?" Emily said, her voice clearly disappointed as she swept back into the kitchen. Had she truly expected us to bolt as soon as she left the room for two minutes?

I had the urge to push back against her plans for us, and said, "You mentioned Cindra is supposed to be here any time now, so we figured we'd just wait." I didn't pause for an answer and instead led the way to the living room and took a seat on the couch.

Tabby followed suit, which I knew she would, and by the time Emily trailed behind us, she was wearing an annoyed scowl. Or was she afraid? Either way, her face held a lot of tension, her forehead and eyebrows pulled tight. She stood over us with her arms crossed.

"Tell me again about your relationship with Melvin Peterson?" Alex had taught me that when he sensed tension in a suspect, that was the time to hit with a hard-hitting question. I wasn't nearly as smooth as he was in this department, but my question clearly rattled the woman.

She heaved out a breath as though my question was exhausting her. "Look, I admit it, okay? I hired you two in order to get the old man riled up a little, but stop looking at me like I'm guilty of anything more than that. I didn't kill him. I wouldn't have a clue how to tinker with electrical wiring. Ask anybody, I would not be capable of rigging a hot tub to kill somebody. I can't even work the television remote."

I twisted my lips. I was tempted to believe her, and wanted to at least confirm this with Victoria, Rhonda, or Cindra. Plus, I wanted to make sure that the police had been the ones to first suggest tampering with the electrical wiring.

Emily's gaze darted from place to place around the big living room before finally landing at the top of the stairs. "Oh, I almost forgot." Her words came out in a strange monotone. "One of your police friends forgot something upstairs in the solarium. I think it's some kind of fancy flashlight."

Tabby popped out of her place on the couch. "I'll grab it, if you want to stay here with Mrs. Peterson." She looked at me with raised eyebrows to make sure this wasn't going to interfere with my plans. The problem was, I didn't really have any plans. I was making this up as I was going along.

But as I nodded, Tabby's smile faded. She touched the green glass at her neck, looked back toward the stairs, and then finally turned to ascend them.

"Are you sure you shouldn't go with her?" Emily's voice was more than tense now. It was filled with fear and even warbled a little as she spoke. But what was she afraid of? Had I hit a nerve with my repeated questions about her relationship with Melvin?

I tried to think of what else I could use as a gauge to see what Emily Peterson was capable of when it came to electrical wiring and damaging a hot tub pump.

As I considered this, a thought occurred to me. "You know, I wonder if my peeler could have gotten stuck somewhere in your dishwasher. Mind if I have a look?" I didn't wait for her response and headed back for the kitchen.

I kneeled in front of their stainless-steel dishwasher and pulled one of the racks all the way forward. "Is there anywhere in here it could have gotten stuck?" I asked, hoping she'd come closer so I could assess her familiarity with at least this appliance.

But she stood at a distance, on the other side of the island, studying her perfectly manicured red nails. "I have no idea. Is there a filter down there or something you could remove?"

There was a filter, but there was no way a utensil could have gotten caught within it. That was obvious from one glance. But the more I thought about it, and the more I looked over prim Emily Peterson with her perfect nails, the more I could not see her tampering with anything mechanical or electrical.

I sighed as I pushed to my feet, ready to go and meet Tabby and get out of here to discuss this all with Alex.

But when I stood, Emily was blocking the door, and holding a very large knife.

Chapter Twenty-seven - Tabby

As I ENTERED THE solarium, I was momentarily distracted by the disassembled hot tub and all the equipment lying around. How would I find the police's forgotten flashlight? Perhaps I should have been the one to try interrogating Emily Peterson while Mallory came up to find it.

The free-standing towel cupboard caught my eye and I raced toward it. The chances that the cryptic treasure hunt was leading me to this particular towel cupboard seemed unlikely, but I had to at least check.

The cupboard had three shelves and it didn't take me long to remove all the towels. I would check them all one by one in a second, but first, I thought I saw a small piece of white paper, barely visible along the back of the bottom white shelf, and it appeared to be taped there.

It didn't help that the lighting in here was dim and had a blue hue, almost like I was underwater. I stood and turned to look for a light switch and just as I did, the door to the solarium slammed. Emily's ultra-tall brother, Benedict stood blocking it. My breath and blood stilled within me at his angry look.

"You couldn't just leave things alone, could you?" he said, in what sounded like a rhetorical question. "You three nosy caterers. Why only two of you today? Where's your third one?"

Third one? Amber? My mind worked fast, and I backed a step away as I told him, "She works at the police station, with forensics, and from what I hear, they have some evidence they are just putting together that will clear everything up."

I wasn't sure how much I could say about this being a murder, but then it seemed Benedict—or Benny—already knew, because he actually started laughing and said, "There were a hundred people who wanted Melvin Peterson dead. It doesn't matter if I did it, because neither me nor my sister are going down for it. Before you so rudely interrupted us, I was busy making certain to plant a few suspicious tools in Cindra's bedroom. Believe me, I've covered my bases."

My eyes widened. Had he just admitted to murdering Melvin Peterson and framing Cindra for it?

"Why did you kill him?" At the same time as asking this, I snuck a hand into my pocket and fiddled for my phone, wondering how I could get a recording app going without looking at the screen.

But I was too obvious. His gaze darted to my pocket and in two swift steps, he had me by the arm. I shrieked, loudly, but he only laughed again.

"That glass there? Those are polycarbonate panels. Plus, the wall to the rest of the house is double insulated with a cement surround. No one will hear you in here, sweetheart." The way he used the nickname made my stomach sour.

He yanked my hand from my pocket, and because I was still holding my phone, it came out with my hand.

"I'll take that." He kept hold of my arm, too tightly, with one hand and twisted it up behind my back so every time I moved, it put me in pain. Then he single-handedly disassembled my phone and pulled the sim card and battery from it. This was definitely a man who was well familiar with how electronics, and probably electricity, functioned. As he worked I tried to yank free from him, but he was too strong and his fingers dug into my arm where I was certain they would leave bruises.

Finally, he dropped the phone to the floor and pocketed the two small items.

Then he grabbed me by both arms and backed me up against the now-empty hot tub. "And as for why, I'll tell you exactly why." As he loomed over me, I could smell his acidic breath. "The old geezer was going to push us out of this house if I didn't do something. First, he told my wife Marissa over and over again she was too good for me. She finally left me and he hired one of his fancy lawyers to make sure I didn't get a cent from her. My sister thought putting him in a nursing home would be enough, but I knew better. I found the paperwork about his contingencies to get us booted out and left with nothing. Once he realized how close Emily and I are, he felt threatened and didn't want us around. He had to go, and he was ready to go anyway. I just helped him along a little."

A doorbell chimed through what must have been ceiling mounted speakers. He wasn't kidding about this room being soundproof, as I didn't hear a single sound through the solarium's door.

Could it be Alex? But, no. He was going to meet us at Mallory's house. He was probably there waiting for us right now.

Benedict swore under his breath and then pulled out his own phone to check the screen. He swore again, to himself, and then said to me, "I have to go deal with something. I'll be back for you in a few minutes." He pushed me back hard against the hot tub. "Now don't you go tampering with the wiring while I'm gone." He let out an evil sounding chuckle, and winked, clearly a threat. "I hear it can be deadly."

As he reached for the door handle, I rushed at him, knowing he would have some way of locking me in here. "I'll just get Mallory and get out of your hair," I said, shouting the words and hoping she might hear me while the door was open.

But once again, he pushed me back and as I fell on my behind, he said, "It's too late for that."

And I knew it was because he had just admitted to murder.

The second he was gone and I heard the lock click, I tried to think rationally. Maybe Mallory already got out. Then again, I knew she wouldn't leave me. What did he plan to do to both of us?

I studied the lock of the door. It had a keyhole and must have had one on the other side as well. I hadn't brought a purse so I patted my pockets and my hair, searching for something I could use to try and pick it. Nothing. I looked around the solarium, down at the disassembled pump and wiring, but Benedict had instilled too much fear into me about what could happen if I touched any of it.

Next, I looked for something that might break the glass. I was only on the second floor, but with the high ceilings of the first floor, it would be a long way down. Still, I'd rather break a bone than be stuck here waiting for whatever Benedict had planned for me. Besides, he could be hurting Mallory right this second. I had to get out and go for help.

I grabbed for the nearest brass towel rack and put all my strength behind it to ram it toward a floor-to-ceiling window that overlooked their backyard.

But the towel rack only bounced back, almost hitting me in the face. My eyes widened. He had said it was unbreakable glass, hadn't he?

I'd been in dangerous situations before, but always with Jay, Aaron, and Sherlock at hand. I grasped for my sea glass, but my magic still wasn't working. Plus, I had no idea what Benedict planned for Mallory downstairs.

My breath hitched on a sob and I forced myself to breathe deeply. What would Jay do if he were here? Or Pepper? Would I ever get back to them in Crystal Cove?

I fisted my hands and stood up straight. I couldn't think like that. I had no one else to depend on, so it was up to me to figure out something.

Now, what did I have to work with?

Chapter Twenty-eight - Alex

I was sure it had been half an hour since Mallory texted. I'd been sitting in her driveway with the car running so Hunter wouldn't freeze in the backseat, but he'd been whining every few minutes, wanting to go inside and see his friends.

"They're not in there," I told him for what had to have been the twentieth time. Grabbing for another file folder, I opened it and tried to get caught up on paperwork by the dim interior car light.

My phone chimed through my Bluetooth speaker and I reached for it, assuming it must be Mallory. But one glance at the display told me it instead was the most dreaded person in my life.

"Hello, Captain," I said in way of an answer.

"Where are you?" Captain Corbett grumbled. "I've been looking all over the station for you."

"Just finishing up an interview." My words always came out too fast when I was stretching the truth. I pulled my seatbelt on and prepared to drive back to the station just as soon as I was off the phone.

"You're heading back here now?" he confirmed.

I let out an inward sigh and was about to tell him yes, when I swore I saw movement from within Mallory's house. She'd have let me know if she was already home, wouldn't she?

"Martinez?" Corbett asked, as I still hadn't answered him.

In two seconds, my mind computed that I was definitely not seeing Mallory inside in the dark. I likely wasn't seeing Tabby or Amber either.

"I think I'm just witnessing a code 146, Captain." I was glad to not have to lie at least about this. I was pretty sure someone had broken into Mallory's house again. "I'll report back in as soon as I can." With that, I hung up on my police captain, which was not normally protocol, even in an emergency situation, but I couldn't help myself. I was too eager to see who had broken into Mallory's house this time, and did it have something to do with the Peterson case?

"Come on, Hunter." I held up his vest and shook it a little. "Apparently, we have work to do."

Once in his vest, Hunter moved silently down the snowy driveway, which hadn't been shoveled again since this evening's snowfall. Mallory had given me a key a couple of months ago, so I pulled it out and tried to keep the rest of my keys silent as I approached the front door.

I cringed when the lock clunked, and then again when the door creaked. I paused to take in any moving shadows, but Hunter didn't. He knew exactly where we were going, and apparently it was the kitchen.

I tiptoed behind him and he stopped and waited for me at the swinging kitchen door. I pushed it open a couple of inches to see Cindra Peterson moving around the kitchen touching chairs and the table and various other objects around the room. I could tell immediately what she was up to. She didn't think we'd fingerprinted the place yet, and after Mallory was asking after the saffron spice grinder, she was here to try and cover her tracks.

All in one motion, I flicked on the light switch and moved into the open kitchen. She froze like a rabbit under a scope and stared at me with wide eyes.

"Where's Mallory and Tabby?" She looked on either side of me, like they may have accompanied me inside. Hunter took several steps forward until he was near enough to sniff Cindra's coat.

"You tell me," I said, still concerned that they were taking so long and suddenly being hit with the idea that perhaps Cindra knew more than she was letting on.

She shrugged and then continued her trek around the kitchen, touching counters and canisters as she went. It seemed she was trying to get away from Hunter, too. In my experience, people only did that when they were allergic, afraid of dogs, or had done something very, very wrong.

"You're here to cover your tracks, aren't you?" I didn't leave her time to answer. "Did you break in to leave the spice grinder here to tip us off?"

Cindra widened her eyes, but the surprise looked fake. "Break in? What are you talking about?"

"The same way you broke in today?" I raised my eyebrows, not letting her out of answering honestly.

Cindra turned away, realizing I could read her perfectly. "What? I was supposed to meet Mallory here. She must have left the door unlocked for me. I never—"

I cut her off. "Save your breath. Mallory never leaves her house unlocked. I'm certain about that and the way you're walking around touching things, my bet is that you're here to cover up your original fingerprints. But it's too late. Forensics has already taken all the fingerprints that are to be found around here."

I only had her in side profile, but she paled at my words.

"If you really want to prove you never broke in, how about I take you down to the police station right now and you can prove your fingerprints don't match any of the ones we lifted this morning."

Her head darted around toward the sliding glass door and then toward the kitchen exit. "I—I can't. I'm late for something with my stepmom." She took a step toward the kitchen door.

"Wait, Cindra. Hang on." I could always get Hunter's help to detain her if I needed to, but I didn't think that would be necessary. "I'll go easier on you if you tell me the truth, but I need to know why you did it. Listen, we found grease on the back door. It wasn't hard to reach the conclusion that you had been the one in here. The saffron grinder is the one from your house, the one that usually sits on your dining room table every single night and is now missing. So who are you trying to lead us to? Your dad? He's the one who likes saffron. Emily? She's the one you don't seem to like. Victoria? She's the one who is in charge of the kitchen tools. Rhonda? She's the one who may have taken the spice grinder to refill it. Who, exactly, are you trying to get us to blame for your grandfather's death and why?"

"Death? No!" Cindra flapped her hands to the sides. "I don't know! Don't you think I want to know more than anybody who killed Gramps? I only set up the treasure hunt for Amber as a fun challenge, like we used to do in school. I haven't really had any friends since high school and I'm not good at that stuff. When I heard Emily hired Amber's catering company, I don't know. I guess I thought it was fate finally helping me out or something." She instantly looked embarrassed by admitting this and changed topics. "Amber said she and Mallory were some kind of amazing sleuths so when I found the saffron grinder in a strange spot, it gave me the idea to hide something Amber had wanted years ago and then drop some clues toward it."

"Are you telling me you leaving the saffron grinder under Mallory's tree had nothing to do with the fact that the blade from it was used to electrocute your grandfather?"

"Are you serious?" Her eyes widened even further, and as Hunter sat back on his haunches, I didn't get the sense she was feigning innocence. "That's why I found it shoved in the towel closet in the solarium," she said, almost to herself. "Someone must have removed the blade and then stashed the grinder where they thought no one would find it for days or even weeks."

I stood there stunned for a long moment. It was an understatement to say this was the most emotion I had seen out of Cindra.

"You have no idea who would have wanted to electrocute your grandfather?" I confirmed.

She let out a humorless laugh. "I know plenty of people who would have probably wanted to."

"But no idea who actually did it?" I finished for her. So his death really was a shock to her. "You didn't act too surprised when Mallory and Tabby told you about his death last night," I said.

Cindra dropped onto a kitchen chair and raked her hands through her short dark hair. "I heard Emily's scream and went to see what it was all about. When Dad was in the hallway comforting her, I heard him say Gramps wanted to die quickly. Then the second everyone finally left the solarium, I had to go in and check for myself. I remembered what Dad said, and I worried that Gramps may still be suffering and nobody could see it, so I unhooked the life preserver, knowing he wouldn't want to come back in even more pain." She held out her hands, as though I might arrest her for this.

"And then you came downstairs, but you still didn't tell anyone that you thought there might be foul play," I said.

She dropped her arms. "I was trying to figure out how to say it. Then when Mallory told me she had some bad news, I kept searching for a way that didn't sound like I should have figured it out and failed him. It's why I said the same thing that my dad said, about Gramps not wanting to suffer. I was trying not to let it show how much I was beating myself up for not taking Emily's threat more seriously."

"Emily's threat?" I asked. Hunter stood up, hearing the concern in my voice.

"I heard Emily telling Benny that she was determined to put the old man in a nursing home. Benny said she would never be able to get him to agree to it, and the nursing home wouldn't admit him against his will. Emily made a stupid joke about pushing him down the stairs and calling it a 'fall', so they'd be able to say he was going senile and admit him no matter what he wanted. I used to think Benny was the only good thing about that family, but he's just like her. I went back into the kitchen before I heard any more and before either of them saw me."

"That family?" I asked.

"Well, yeah. He's her brother. And their parents ditched them both when they were young, so they're super protective over each other." Before Cindra's next words came out of her mouth, I put it together in my head. "But most people call him Benedict."

I had wanted to interview all of the family members last night, and when I asked Emily Peterson if there were any other relatives, she had shaken her head and said everyone other than Cindra and her husband had just been there as party guests. I made notes about Benedict and noticed one other point I hadn't followed through on. "What item did you hide for Amber to find?"

Cindra shook her head. "It was nothing. Just a stupid steel star that the teacher made us compete for back in welding class. In truth, Amber should have won it because she worked really hard on a complicated project that was too advanced for her. I just made this stupid barbecue spatula that I could have made in my sleep. But I shouldn't have put my effort into setting up the treasure hunt. If I'd taken a minute to think of how strange it was to find the spice grinder in that closet..."

I waited her out as she took a deep breath. Then another. Finally, she went on, "I'm pretty sure I know who killed my gramps. That's why I came back here tonight to tell Mallory."

The creases of her forehead told me she was telling the truth about all of it. "Who do you think killed your grandfather?"

"Emily and her brother."

I knew Cindra had a chip on her shoulder about her stepmother Emily, but I sensed this was more than a personal vendetta.

"I always used to like Benny, back when he was married to Marissa. But after she left him, something changed. She hired some bigwig lawyer and left him with nothing. He was convinced that the same thing was going to happen to Emily."

I twisted my lips, thinking. "Mallory and Tabby were supposed to be back half an hour ago. They were at your house, trying to get some answers."

Cindra's gaze stayed steady on mine. "Emily must be there by now. I was supposed to go to a book signing with her tonight. I'll bet Benny's there, too, and if Mallory and Tabby are asking too many questions, well, they could be in serious trouble."

Chapter Twenty-nine - Mallory

"IF YOU'RE LOOKING AT anybody right now, you should be looking at that big problem just waiting to happen, Cindra," Emily said, waving the knife around in a way that made me want to duck.

"Do you think she would have done something to hurt her grandfather?" I asked. It was too late to pussyfoot around the topic.

She huffed. "You know teenagers. They don't care about anyone else except themselves." It was clearly Emily's aim to throw Cindra under the bus any way she could in order to get attention off of her.

I hoped Tabby would return soon, because I didn't love the crazed look in Emily's eyes as she swung the knife around.

The doorbell rang and I expected Emily to put the knife down to go and answer it, but instead, she took two steps closer toward me, the knife now held up like a weapon above me she intended to use.

Footsteps sounded from the stairwell, but they sounded heavy. Too heavy to be Rhonda or Victoria. A second later, Benedict poked his head into the kitchen. He took one look at the knife in Emily's hand and... nodded, like he was pleased.

"Why is that child ringing the doorbell?" Benedict asked his sister.

Emily's forehead creased. "Cindra? She's outside?" Her voice trembled with her questions. "She must have forgotten her keys again. Are you sure it's her?"

Benedict nodded. "I saw her through the living room window." As if on cue, the doorbell rang again.

"What do we do?" Emily asked, now waving the knife so close to my face, I had to pull back.

"It's cold outside. Shouldn't you let her in?" I asked. It was all I could come up with to try and play dumb, like I didn't know that these two were clearly dangerous.

Emily waved a hand—thankfully the one that did not hold the knife. "She's forgotten her keys before. She'll think I already left and go to the bookstore. Just give it a minute."

The doorbell rang a third time and all three of us looked up to the ceiling where the sound emanated from.

After a silent pause, Benedict said, "I'll check."

He was back less than a minute later, but when he entered the kitchen and said, "You're right. She's gone," it startled Emily and she came just short of lunging toward me with the knife.

"Oh, Benny! It's you." Emily threw a hand to her chest. "You dealt with the other one, right?" Her voice still had that trembling quality. When she motioned toward the front room, it occurred to me she was talking about Tabby.

But I barely had time to worry over her when Benedict said, "I'm dealing with her," and grabbed for my arm. "I'll deal with them together." He pushed me toward the door and said, "You just get the employees out of here. Give them the night off and tell them you want the house to yourself. This time, we're not leaving any loose ends. We'll dispose of the bodies somewhere far away from your house."

Bodies? I opened my mouth to scream, but before any sound left me, Benedict's hand clamped tightly over my mouth.

"It won't be my house much longer if anyone finds out," Emily said, as if that was the problem.

"No one will find out," was the last thing I heard as Benedict practically dragged me through the door and up the stairs.

We reached the solarium, and I was still trying to yank away from Benedict and kick at him, but the man had a lot of strength behind that seven-foot frame.

As he used a key to unlock the door, I prayed that Tabby was still okay and that maybe we'd find a way to save each other from this mad brother/sister duo.

The instant he opened the door, I saw Tabby all the way across the solarium by the floor-to-ceiling windows. I wondered if she'd tried to break them. It couldn't be too far to the ground.

As soon as she saw us, she spun and ran straight at us. Or, rather, straight at Benedict. He rammed me sideways into the doorframe and then stopped her as though she was a tiny housefly. Then he pushed her backward until she fell down and tossed me like a rag doll through the door and on top of her.

"My sister is making sure no one will bother us," he gritted through his teeth, proving he actually had been winded by our fight. "Scream all you want in here, and then I'll be back to deal with you once and for all."

Chapter Thirty - Tabby

"ALEX IS OUTSIDE," I told Mallory as I caught my breath and righted myself. "This room is soundproof, but he knows we're up here. I saw him calling for backup."

"What if Benedict returns before backup gets here?" Mallory pushed to her feet and rushed to the window. She shook her head. "I don't see Alex."

"He's out there somewhere. I saw him right down there." I pointed below the window. "You stay here. If Benedict returns, I'll be by the door, ready to yell."

Mallory shook her head. "Emily is getting rid of the staff, and she's in on it with him."

"Then I'll have to attack him and Emily. The only chance we have is taking them by surprise."

Mallory's forehead creased. "I don't like this, Tabby. Emily had a knife!"

Had Emily been downstairs threatening Mallory with a knife? I didn't like this idea either, but I didn't know that we had a choice and I hoped I'd be able to protect us with the small steel star I'd found taped to the ceiling. When nothing had broken the window, I'd returned to the towel closet and gotten a look at the note taped to the bottom shelf. It read: IF YOU FIND THIS, IT'S CLEAR IT WAS IN THE STARS FOR YOU TO WIN.

I'd first looked outside, and that was when I'd seen Alex, but then the silver star taped to the ceiling caught my eye and I'd climbed up the towel closet to get it. I was expecting another clue, but when there wasn't one, I pocketed the star in hopes it might at least serve as a weapon of protection.

What seemed like only seconds later, Benedict returned. The instant he opened the door, I used all my voice to scream "Help!" to the staff who may still be in the mansion somewhere, and all my strength to rush at him and jump onto his back from right at the side of the door.

I grasped the steel star tightly in my hand as I glimpsed Hunch shoot in behind the tall man. The star was only about two inches wide and I thought I had a good grip on it, but he had a giant kitchen knife in his hand and as he swung it back toward me, it only missed my arm by a fraction of an inch and the star flew out of my hand.

In an instant, Mallory was on the move, but even together, I didn't know if we could get the knife away from this man without getting seriously injured or even killed.

Chapter Thirty-one – Alex

I WAS ALMOST AROUND the large house and out of the backyard when Mallory suddenly appeared in the solarium windows, frantically waving her arms. Hunter let out a low growl at my side and I patted his head.

"I know," I told my dog. "I think she's in trouble, too."

Cindra clomped through the snow around the side of the house. "They wouldn't even open the door for me. Something's going on in there that they don't want anyone to know about."

I nodded, my pulse ratcheting up from sudden worry. "I think you're right. Good plan, pretending to have forgotten your keys. Do you have a key for the back door, too?" As I spoke, I kicked snow out of my way and passed the four-car garage.

By the time I got to the mudroom door, Cindra was behind me, pushing a key into my hands. I fumbled it into the lock and relief washed over me as it clicked open. Pushing open the door, I didn't take time to check if Cindra was behind me as I slopped my slushy boots through the mudroom, into the kitchen, and then through the living room, frantically looking around for anything or anyone who might stop my progress toward Mallory.

Hunter went first and had made it halfway up the stairs before I'd looked up at where he'd paused.

Emily Peterson was in the middle of the stairway with wide eyes, looking between me and the dog that had her backed up against the railing, sniffing her. A loud growl of a sound emanated from the direction of the solarium, and when I recognized Mallory's voice behind it, I launched up the stairs three at a time to get to her.

In my concern, it was hard to remember which way to go in the maze of upper hallways, but I said, "Find Mallory!" to my dog and he bounded past me to lead the way.

By the time I caught up to him in the solarium doorway, it seemed I was almost unnecessary. Tabby was on

Benedict's back, holding one of his arms, while Hunch hung from his other arm, claws dug in. Mallory stood a foot away, wielding a large kitchen knife in one hand and a small silver star in the other.

But it seemed I was necessary after all, because my dog let out one loud bark at the scene and Hunch released from Benedict's arm and took off like a bolt of lightning past me. Hunter, still a puppy at heart, started barking wildly, his head swinging around as he struggled between holding fast to the perpetrator or chasing a cat.

I stepped up beside him and held one hand on his head to calm him as I flashed my badge with the other and told the tall man, "You have the right to remain silent."

Tabby slid off of his back and I had him by the arm when suddenly Cindra called, "Help! She's getting away!"

Now that I was sure I had Benedict under control, I turned my attention to Hunter. "Go get her, boy!"

He launched out of the room, and we followed behind—right after I got my handcuffs locked around Benedict's wrists.

We headed downstairs and then out into the snow toward my police car. It wasn't difficult to spot Hunter where he had Emily pinned down in the snow.

Chapter Thirty-two – Tabby

TWO DAYS LATER, I packed my luggage, placing my new vegetable slicer right on top. I knew every time I used it, I would think of my visit to Honeysuckle Grove and all we had gone through together.

"Tabby, what can I make you for the road?" Amber called from downstairs. I had been teaching her how to make specialty coffees over the last two days as we tried to decompress from all we had been through, even though extra caffeine probably wasn't what any of us truly needed.

"How about a half-sweet decaf caramel latte?" I called back, emphasizing the decaffeinated part. I hoped to get a little sleep on the plane ride back to Oregon.

When I arrived at the bottom of the stairs, she was there to serve it to me in a to-go cup. Hunch moved toward me and rubbed up against my shins.

"He's warmed up to you," Amber observed.

I reached down to pet him but didn't want to chance picking him up just yet. Maybe I'd try that on my next visit. "I should be purring and offering my love to him. He saved our lives, after all." If not for Hunch, Mallory and I wouldn't have had a chance of getting the large knife out of Benedict's hands without getting seriously injured. That fearless cat had jumped at the weapon and dug his claws into the man's arm like he was ready to sacrifice his own life to save us.

Amber chuckled and lifted Hunch into her arms, cradling him like a baby. "That's what you do best, isn't it, Hunchie?" I still had no idea how Amber got away with the cutesy nickname, not to mention the cuddling.

Soon, the four of us were off toward the airport—Mallory, Amber, Hunch, and me. Amber drove, like last time, but it hadn't snowed in a couple of days so the roads were much clearer. I'd said goodbye to Alex the night before when he'd come over for some of Mallory and Amber's wonderful biscuits and gravy.

"Should I stop at the store for pepperoni rolls?" Amber asked us.

Mallory rolled her eyes. "All you ever think about is food."

Even though I wasn't sure if Mallory actually wanted to stop, I couldn't help myself. I said. "I could go for a pepperoni roll to get me through the long travel day."

With that, it was decided, and soon the front cab of the catering van smelled like doughy, spicy goodness.

"Are both Benedict and Emily going to jail?" I asked when we were back on the road. I always asked Jay questions like this after we had wrapped up a case, but I hadn't felt quite as free bringing up my queries with Alex. We hadn't had much chance to talk when we hadn't been either investigating a murder or trying to get out of danger.

Amber was the one to nod and answer. "It'll take a while for them to get scheduled for trial, but so far they haven't had anyone spring for bail for them. I don't see them getting out anytime soon, and my hope is that they get some psychiatric help on top of jail time."

The young girl sure knew a lot about the judicial system.

I sighed and chewed another bite of my pepperoni roll. I'd been planning to save it for the plane, but apparently that wasn't going to happen. "What do you think about spending some time with Cindra?"

"Yeah, Alex mentioned something about that. Part of me wonders if she's too much like me for a friendship to work, but, honestly, it's probably healthy for me to at least have one friend my age. We're meeting for coffee this week."

I got the sense that Amber rarely showed much hope or positivity about these kinds of things, but it pleased me she was giving Cindra a chance. It even seemed to please my sea glass, which gave a sudden, unexpected pulse of warmth.

I had grown so much on this trip, learning to trust Mallory and Amber, and learning to trust my own intuition when I'd had trouble finding any magic. I also had a new outlook on friendship. Sure, it wouldn't always be as effortless as it had been with Mallory, but friendships of all kinds had value in bringing out more of your own unique strengths. Mallory seemed more confident than when I'd first arrived, too, and I felt like I'd helped her grow as well.

Our visit was exhausting, but worth the effort in so many ways. "I feel like I need a vacation from my vacation," I joked.

Mallory and Amber chuckled. Then Mallory got serious. "I'm sorry this ended up being such a stressful time."

I shook my head. "I'm glad I was here to help. Just promise me our next visit won't be quite so adventurous."

Amber glanced away from the road so I could catch the gleam in her eye. Today, her sweatshirt declared in big bold letters: SUNSHINE, MIXED WITH A LITTLE HURRICANE.

"Oh, Tabby. Have you met us?" she asked. "We can't promise that."

Mallory nudged her in the side and then turned to me. "But we can promise we will try to see you again soon, right, Amber? Maybe a real vacation all together? Somewhere tropical and not full of knee-deep snow?"

That sounded like a dream about now. I let my mind go, thinking if my sister Pepper and Jay could join us somewhere, not to mention Alex...

"Let's do it!" I said, too excited not to. "Let's plan a vacation somewhere as soon as Amber is free from school and her internship."

With that, it was settled. We would see each other again, and maybe next time our visit wouldn't be upended by a murder investigation.

Then again, with all of us in the same room... maybe it would.

The End

Would you like to read on in either the Mallory Beck Cozy Culinary Capers or the Tabitha Chase Days of the Week Mysteries? Turn the page for a sneak peek of both!

Sneak Peek - Murder at Mile Marker 18 (Book 1 in the Mallory Beck Cozy Culinary Capers)

Chapter One

THE WIFE OF A war correspondent or a fighter pilot or even a venomous snake milker (yes, there is such a thing) might expect to be a widow at twenty-eight, but certainly not the wife of a novelist.

And yet here I was, learning how to live life in the oversized house, in a small West Virginia town we settled into only a year ago—alone. To be fair, I hadn't done much in the way of living in the last eight months since Cooper died, but after an offhand comment from my sister about me being under great threat of becoming a cat lady, I was determined to start today.

Being a cat lady wouldn't be so bad if the cat I'd inherited didn't loathe me.

I swung my legs out of Cooper's black Jeep and did a little hip shimmy to straighten my skirt as I stood. Picking out clothes this morning had been about as difficult as choosing between cake and pie (no one should ever have to make that choice). What does one wear that says, I'm fine, just fine, and I haven't been moping around my dark house for the last eight months, nope, not me, but nonetheless, please, keep your distance?

Even though it was the middle of August, I had settled on a black skirt with the tiniest of polka dots and a light cornflower blue blouse with matching pumps and a headband that pulled my in-need-of-a-trim bangs back. It didn't spell out the last eight months of my life, but it did the job in making me feel tidy and unapproachable. My coffee-brown hair fell halfway down my back now, full of split ends, but it actually didn't look half bad today for how many months it had been matted against my living room couch.

I strode for the church, the same one I hadn't stepped foot inside since Cooper's memorial service. Church had always been Cooper's thing. I'd gone along to play the part of the good wife but didn't spend too much time considering how I felt about God or how

He felt about me. At least I hadn't before He decided to snatch my husband from me.

Two greeters in their mid-forties stood at the closest open glass doors—a man in a gray suit and a woman in an apricot summer dress. Thankfully, I didn't recognize either of them. I'd chosen this as my first big public outing because, at more than three hundred people, I figured our church was the one place I might get in and out of completely unnoticed. As I approached the greeters, though, the woman leaned into the man and whispered something.

I gulped. Apparently, this was how it would go: People would recognize me, remember Cooper, and not know what to say. Why, again, had I gotten out of bed this morning? There had to be at least one Netflix series I hadn't binged yet.

The woman at the door pasted on a bright smile as she turned back to me, just in time to say, "Good morning."

"Good morning," I murmured back, but my voice came out hard and crusty, like bread out of a too-hot oven, or like I hadn't used it in more than a week. Come to think of it, other than talking on the phone with my sister, I probably hadn't. My tone, at least, had the desired effect, and the greeters let me pass without another word.

My next goal was to make it through the lobby and into the sanctuary without garnering any other stares or attention. This part was not easy. All eyes followed me as I entered the church lobby, and I was pretty sure I wasn't just imagining it.

My late husband, Cooper Beck, had been a well-known mystery writer, so I was used to recognition. After only five years, I hadn't been married long enough to get used to this feeling of notoriety, and I guess I had assumed it would have died with Cooper.

Apparently not so. And not only that, but every single person nearby was scanning my body, probably taking in my too-bright cornflower blouse and thinking it inappropriate for someone in mourning, or noticing the tiny polka dots on my skirt, or wondering why I still wore black after so many months, or...something.

While I was lost in my warring thoughts, Donna Mayberry spotted me, at first only giving me a glance, and I thought I might make it into the sanctuary before actually having to speak to her. But then she did a double take, quickly followed by the head tilt of pity. By this point, I knew that look well. That look was why I had taken to grocery shopping and running errands at midnight instead of during the day like a normal person. At midnight, I could safely avoid the head tilt of pity.

"Mallory Beck?" Donna called with an arm straight up in the air, so any stray person in the vicinity who hadn't yet set eyes on me might do so now. "It's so nice to see you out!" she said loudly, calling public attention to my self-imposed isolation in only two seconds.

Donna had the kind of long legs that would be impossible to outrun. In fact, I blinked, and she was right there beside me. Donna was long everywhere—from her fingers to the dark, shiny hair that fell past her waist. She wore a summery yellow dress that touched the floor, and I had to wonder what kind of a store made clothes that would look long on someone like nearly six-foot Donna. Whether it was her hair or her stature or her clothes, though, Donna Mayberry always seemed to have a way of making me feel frumpy and underdressed.

Then again, maybe all these people would finally look at her instead of me.

Donna and Marv were one of the first couples Cooper and I had met when we'd settled into Honeysuckle Grove a year ago, and while Marv worked about sixteen hours a day, Donna naturally excelled at everything from shrub carving to Michelangelo-inspired nail design, and seemed to have a little too much time on her hands—time to know everything about everyone.

"How are you doing, honey? Is this your first time back at church?" Again with the head tilt of pity. Even though I doubted Donna could know I hadn't left my house in thirteen days, somehow her tone confirmed she absolutely did.

"First time, yes," I replied. No point in denying it.

She angled me away from the imposing stares and nudged me toward an alcove as though she could sense how much the staring bothered me. A second later, a tall, potted plant concealed us in the corner of the lobby, and I had just let out a breath of relief when Donna suddenly started pulling at my skirt.

I grabbed for my skirt and looked down in horror. Was Donna trying to undress me? Was this a bad dream? Maybe I was still sleeping soundly—or as soundly as one could beside a hostile cat while dreaming about being undressed in public.

But as I blinked and then blinked again, Donna held up a pair of beige control-top pantyhose she had peeled off the outside of my skirt to show me. A second later, she tucked them into the outside pouch of my gray leather purse.

"Oh!" I let out a loud noise, something between a yelp and a laugh. "Thank you!"

As I peeked around the plant, it seemed everyone had lost interest in us, thank goodness.

"Well, you'll have to sit with us." Donna straightened her own dress and looked down as though something equally embarrassing might have happened to her, but I was pretty sure we both knew that wasn't how the universe worked. I doubted Marv was here, so "us" likely meant Donna's gossip posse—that was what Cooper and I used to call them—but as Donna tugged my arm toward the far side of the lobby, a jolt of panic shot through me.

"Oh, I can't," I said, pulling away from her eight-tone sunset nails. "I'm, um, meeting someone, and I said I'd be sitting on this side." The first lie I could think of launched off my tongue. I just couldn't imagine sitting with Donna's posse and having them all whisper, "Yes, but how are you really doing?" fifty times throughout the service.

Donna looked to either side of me as though she might regard this mysterious person I could be waiting for. I could have continued with the lie. Said my sister was in town or conjured an imaginary friend or something to put her mind at rest. But I was suddenly just so tired from all of this interaction—the most I'd endured in eight months—and so I simply stood there staring at Donna like my brain had taken an extended vacation.

Eventually, she said, "Oh. Okay then. If you're sure?"

I nodded as she backed away, leaving me to my social anxiety.

A few more head tilts greeted me as I took my seat near the back of the sanctuary on the right, nice and close to the door. Thankfully, my chosen outfit—sans the sticky pantyhose—did its duty of keeping me mostly unapproachable. The church had rarely filled to capacity when Cooper and I had attended, so I had some confidence I'd have the back bench to myself. The only time I'd actually seen this place full was at Cooper's memorial service, but most of those were mystery fans and people fascinated with death, not people who had actually known him.

Soon, the service started with singing and then the pastor's invitation for people to donate and volunteer in any area they were able. Nothing had changed in eight months, apparently. Honeysuckle Grove Community Church still didn't have enough money in the building fund or enough people to host small group Bible studies in their homes. It seemed so very odd that while my life had been turned on its head, leaving me without a husband or a profession, every person around me seemed like a walking robot, pre-programmed for a life that would remain constant until their pre-determined time of death.

As though Pastor Jeff could read my mind, he started his sermon with, "We are not robots."

That was one thing I'd forgotten about church. Pastor Jeff had a great gift for storytelling. He usually started one of his stories with a bold and unusual statement, and then went on a long rabbit trail about his son's first crack at baseball or about that time he lost his luggage in a Taiwanese airport, but then brought it back around to that first bold statement in a way that made the entire congregation think, Ah, I see what you did there!

But today, I feared I didn't have the brain capacity to follow his breadcrumbs. He chattered on about what it meant to be part of a family and body parts working together and covering a multitude of sins. At least I had been correct about getting the back bench to myself.

I tuned out for a minute, or maybe it was more than a minute, because the next thing I knew, Pastor Jeff closed his Bible and bowed his head to pray.

I'd done it! I'd made it through the entire service. Okay, maybe I hadn't taken much of it in, but I'd spoken to an actual person, I'd sat here and proved I could act normal, and I hadn't drawn a single bit of attention to myself. Well, besides the part where I wore my pantyhose on the outside of my skirt.

"I'm sorry to have to tell you there's been a recent death in the congregation," Pastor Jeff said. At first, I expected all eyes to once again turn to me, but then quickly realized "recent" in Pastor Jeff's books meant something during the last two seasons. "This past Friday, August the thirteenth, Dan Montrose met his death in an unfortunate accident."

Pastor Jeff resumed bowing his head to pray for the family and their loss. His deep voice boomed with emotion and instantly made me feel like I'd gone back in time eight months. I could physically feel grief for this family I'd never even met, like a two-hundred-pound anchor in my stomach. Pastor Jeff went on to talk about the shock of the death and the wife and children this man had left behind, and because I couldn't bear the weight of the extra grief, I kept my eyes open and focused on our authoritative, if somewhat frazzled, pastor.

Pastor Jeff wore jeans and a beige button-down today. His hair was more in need of a trim than mine, which was saying something, but in every bit of his countenance, he oozed compassion. I wondered how overworked Pastor Jeff must be to take care of such a large congregation. It must involve a lot of stress for someone who cared so much. After Cooper died, Pastor Jeff visited me three times at the house, until I'd finally donned a face that convinced him I was doing fine, just fine, and didn't need a fourth visit. In truth, I probably did need that fourth visit, but even then, in the midst of my grief, I had somehow inherently known that I would be doing our overworked pastor a great favor by letting him move on to some other hurting soul within the church.

"Anyone?" Pastor Jeff said, and it took me a second to realize he had finished praying and now gazed over the congregation with his eyes pleading, as he often did at the beginning of the service when asking for volunteers. I had tuned out again. "Can anyone be the arms of this church body and deliver a casserole to these hurting folks, to help out this part of our church family?" He scanned the entire congregation a second time. "It doesn't have to be anything fancy."

He looked to the far side of the sanctuary where Donna and her gossip posse huddled whispering, and then in front of them to where the rest of the church staff sat. The church secretary, Penny Lissmore, let out such a large breath of disappointment, I could see her chest heave from across the large worship center. Pastor Jeff sighed as though admitting defeat to her and explaining telepathically that they'd have to add Casserole Delivery to the long list of things someone on the staff would eventually have to get to.

After Cooper died, I'd had at least a couple of casseroles delivered to me. That time was a bit of a haze, and I definitely didn't ponder at the time how much cajoling it might have taken to get someone to pick up a casserole at the store—they were the store-bought variety, I remembered that much—and bring it over to my house.

I got it. Approaching a grieving widow was probably near the bottom of most people's lists of favorite things to do, right below getting a root canal or having a wardrobe malfunction on your first day back at church. But for the first time, I understood how comforting those little acts of kindness could be.

While I was lost in my thoughts again, I didn't immediately notice the church secretary and an associate pastor look my way, followed by Pastor Jeff. His face broke into a smile that looked as though heaven had just opened and angels were descending right here on this side of the sanctuary.

"Mallory Beck!" he said, and I startled at my name. "I knew I could count on you. Thank you so much, Mallory. The Montrose family will really appreciate this."

I blinked as I clued in to what he was saying. And that's when I realized my hand was high in the air.

Chapter Two

Two hours later, I stumbled through my front door, carrying more groceries than one person should be able to manage. As if to prove my point, as I kicked the door shut behind me, the bottom fell out of one of the brown paper bags in my right arm, and dried noodles scattered everywhere.

Hunch peeked around the corner to investigate. Cooper's cat generally snubbed his nose in my direction. Once in a while, he greeted me with a hiss—usually when I was already having a particularly bad day. My sister, Leslie, thought I should really take Hunch down to the SPCA if we didn't get along, but I couldn't get rid of Cooper's beloved cat. Of course I couldn't.

But we also couldn't stand each other.

Now he looked up at me as if saying, "This is new," about not only the noodles on the floor, but also about my overloaded arms. Generally, when I made a trip to the grocery store, I returned with one bag, maybe two. It didn't take a lot to feed a single person, especially one who rarely remembered to eat. Or a single person and a mourning cat.

Yes, mourning. I should take a step back and explain. You see, Hunch was not a normal cat. Hunch's personality was more dog-like than feline in many ways, and he had been every bit the ideal mystery writer's companion. The cat had only ever seemed to enjoy Cooper's company, and I hadn't taken it personally when Cooper was alive because they clearly fit together. When Cooper paced, Hunch paced right alongside him. When Cooper came up with a great plot idea and snapped his fingers, Hunch perched on his haunches right at Cooper's side to high five his owner. I kid you not. Or in this case, would you call it a low five?

I still didn't take Hunch's bristly nature to heart. It just disappointed me that we both missed Cooper terribly and yet we couldn't comfort each other through our grief.

But I could never fill the void Cooper had left in Hunch's life. I couldn't possibly stir up the kind of creative energy that new mysteries and their solutions brought with them. I'd been reading Cooper's novels nonstop for six months to keep what little he'd left behind close to me, and all it had taught me was that I'd lost someone brilliant. No wonder he'd had such a large fan base.

I dropped the intact grocery bags onto the kitchen counter and returned to clean up my mess. Hunch was still investigating, sniffing every inch of my torn grocery bag and its contents like a squatty feline bloodhound. He looked up at me and I swear he raised his eye whiskers on one side as if to ask, "What, exactly, are you up to?"

"I wish I was up to something more exciting," I told Hunch. Cooper had often talked to his cat, but for me, it had always felt strange, at least before today. "Just cooking up a casserole for some nice people who recently experienced a death in the family."

Hunch's fur pricked up on the word "death" and even though there was no story here, no mystery about what I planned to concoct in the kitchen, I figured it wouldn't hurt to let Hunch think differently.

"I'll have to figure out what to do now that I've wasted my noodles," I said, pacing a few times back and forth in our entryway and drumming my fingers on my chin. Hunch watched me for a few seconds. And then he joined me.

The truth was, I knew exactly what to do. And, in fact, purchasing the dried pasta noodles had been a cop-out on my part—barely a step above buying a frozen lasagna.

I didn't blame anyone else for opting for store-bought, of course. Other people had busy lives, while I had absolutely nothing on my agenda, besides getting out of bed and pouring a bowl of cat kibble. Also, most other people didn't have a culinary degree.

Half an hour later, my oven pinged to let me know it was preheated, but I still hadn't decided on a recipe. I had all the ingredients for a basic pasta recipe, but basic seemed much too boring when I hadn't had the opportunity to cook for anyone in eight months. I'd bought tomatoes, so I could flavor the pasta that way, but it still didn't seem good enough. Why hadn't I picked up some spinach? Maybe some saffron?

It ended up being three days and four trips to the grocery store later when I finally decided on a recipe I was happy with. I'd fried sauces and taste-tested a dozen different cheeses. I knew beyond any doubt that I was putting far too much thought into this, and yet I couldn't seem to stop myself.

Besides, once the casserole was cooked, that meant I had to actually deliver it.

But by Wednesday, I had finally worked up the courage and got out of bed by seven in the morning to get started—a time of the day I hadn't seen in many months.

Once again, I preheated the oven, mixed eggs, flour, and salt, and separated my dough into three balls. I blended my first ball with a dough hook and a cup of pureed spinach, the second with crushed tomato, and the third with some olive oil and a touch of saffron. By the time I rolled them all out onto my counter and sliced them into thin fettuccine noodles, I was perfectly pleased with the bouquet of edible colors.

Hunch had been lying on his chair at the kitchen table, chin on his paws, since I started. His eyes followed me throughout the kitchen as I asked myself questions aloud about my recipe and then answered them as if each one were a clue in a grand mystery.

For the first time in eight months, Hunch and I seemed to enjoy each other's company, and all at once, something felt very right about this decision to make a meal for this grieving family. The truth was, I never needed to work again if I didn't want to. Cooper had excellent life insurance, plus a steady stream of royalties from his books. But therein lay the problem—I didn't want to go back to working in a bustling kitchen, and yet I terribly missed cooking, as it never seemed worth putting much effort into the process for only one person. It would be so much easier to stop sitting around my big, lonely house, moping all day every day, if I had somewhere to be.

And now for at least one afternoon, I did.

I continued to ask questions aloud, like, "I wonder how the man died," and "I wonder how his wife is dealing with her grief," as I heated some oil in a saucepan over medium heat, to keep Hunch's attention. I warmed my crushed garlic in the oil until fragrant, added more freshly boiled and crushed tomatoes, and salt. By the time the sauce thickened, I had some chopped basil ready to add.

I grated some cheddar and tried it with the sauce, but quickly decided it lacked richness and added some gorgonzola.

Then I layered the casserole into my best white casserole dish—pasta in three different-flavored mounds, then the sauce, a little extra sea salt, and finally the mixture of grated cheeses. I decorated the top with chopped green and yellow peppers for color.

I popped it into the oven and set it to bake twenty-five minutes. And then I raced upstairs to choose an outfit for today's special outing.

Chapter Three

By eleven o'clock that morning, I stood on the doorstep of a sprawling cornstalk-yellow mansion in the upscale Hillcrest neighborhood of Honeysuckle Grove. Cooper had bought us a large house when we had moved to town—large enough, we'd thought, to fill with a boatload of children one day—but it was situated in the flats and nothing like this mountain of a house.

A four-car garage sat off to the left, with mature trees lining a walkway on either side of the expansive yard, but I headed for the ten-foot-wide marbled steps that led to the front door.

When I'd said goodbye to Hunch from our doorstep, he had been sitting on his haunches in the entryway, and I suspected he would be in that same exact position when I returned, eager to hear what I'd discovered during my outing.

The doorbell let out three long chimes when I pressed on it. A moment later, the heavy oak door creaked open, and a maid with flawless bronze skin stood on the other side. The maid wore an actual bonnet and one of those old-fashioned black dresses with a white apron, but her dress ended mid-thigh—shorter than I'd ever seen on any kind of uniform. With long, dark lashes and high cheekbones, the lady was very pretty and had great legs, so it wasn't surprising she'd want to show them off.

"Um, hi." I held out the casserole, hoping my gesture might say it all, as my casual conversational ability hadn't returned since Cooper's death. But the maid just stood there, staring at me with a blank expression. "I'm delivering a casserole on behalf of Honeysuckle Grove Community Church?" I asked it as a question because now that I thought about it, did these people need or even want my delicately prepared dish if they had a maid and probably a cook who could prepare anything at their whim?

Still, I reasoned, maybe the act of kindness would mean something, even to folks with an unlimited supply of money. You never knew.

I held out the casserole another inch toward the maid and said, "Is Mrs. Montrose at home?" All I'd gotten out of Pastor Jeff in the small amount of conversation I could endure Sunday morning was a last name and an address.

"You know the family?" Her blank stare persisted.

I shifted uncomfortably. "Um, no. Not exactly. I was just bringing this by..."

Quite suddenly, she spun and walked into the mansion, leaving the door wide open. As she strode off, she said, "I see if I find her. There is a velatorio—a wake on right now, you know."

I sucked in a breath. I hadn't known. From the sounds of the woman, a stranger delivering a casserole at this moment was about as inappropriate as bringing a carton of cigarettes to a cancer patient's first chemo treatment. I was torn between racing my casserole back to my vehicle or placing the dish somewhere just inside the doorway before escaping.

Before I'd known these people were wealthy, I'd decided to use a casserole dish Cooper and I had gotten as a wedding gift, figuring the gesture would force me on another outing to come and retrieve it. But I knew without a doubt that I would never show up on this doorstep again in search of my beloved casserole dish. When I tried to picture it, all I could envision was me, draped in rags, holding out my hands, and saying, "Please, ma'am? Alms for the poor?"

The image should have made the decision easy. Back away and save the casserole for yourself, Orphan Mallory. But I was having trouble doing that, and before I could force myself to retreat down the steps, another lady stood in the open doorway.

"Mrs. Montrose?" I asked. All this internal debating had made me breathless.

"Yes?" This lady's face bloomed into a bright smile, and again I doubted whether or not I had the right house, the right family. The lady wore her auburn hair in a big bouffant, like something out of the sixties, but her cream-colored, perfectly-tailored dress looked modern. The cream color made me pause again.

Could this truly be the wife of the deceased?

But more than my curiosity, self-consciousness consumed me as I stood there in my khaki capris with a sleeveless floral blouse that was tied at the waist. My dress was more than inappropriate for a wake.

"I'm so sorry if this is poor timing," I said and, as hard as I fought it, found my head tilting at her. "I'm delivering a casserole on behalf of Honeysuckle Grove Community Church?" As I said the words, a familiarity developed. Had I seen this lady at church before? It had been so long since I'd been a regular attendee, I couldn't be sure.

"Oh, how lovely," the woman said, her smile brightening even more. "Please, do bring it in and put it on the dining table." She opened the door wider. As I stepped inside, she glanced down at the steam-obscured lid and asked, "Does it have gluten? Or dairy?"

I gulped and stopped in place. I stalled, slipping out of my ballet flats as Cooper and I had been in a habit of doing since buying our new home. "Oh. I'm afraid it has both," I finally said.

When I had worked in various restaurants in the city, they had always listed gluten- and dairy-free options on the menu. It helped with the awkwardness of having to revamp recipes. Allergies hadn't even occurred to me during this morning's cooking spree.

Mrs. Montrose moved deeper into the house. I glanced down and noticed she'd left her shoes on, which, now that I thought about it, was probably more common for a wake, wasn't it?

"No matter, the kids will eat it." Mrs. Montrose waved a casual hand back at me as I debated between putting my shoes back on or leaving them behind. I left them behind for fear she'd lose me in her massive house. I was already dressed completely wrong. What was the difference if I was barefoot? As she continued to lead the way, she murmured, "And if they don't eat it, the greedy, bloodsucking leeches will," so low that I didn't know if I was meant to hear it.

Mrs. Montrose led me through an open room filled with mourners—all dressed in black with either what looked like a mimosa or a fancy canapé in hand—and through to a dining room filled with more food than I had ever seen in one place—and I had worked in more than one restaurant!

The oversized dining room table didn't have an inch of free space. Mrs. Montrose surveyed it quickly, flashed another smile back at me, and said, "Not to worry, I'll call Lupe to help. Lupe?" She pushed through a swinging door and returned a second later with the short-skirted maid on her heels. "Please help Miss...?"

This seemed like an opportunity to be an ear of understanding to these people, so I took it. "Actually, it's Mrs.," I said. "Mrs. Mallory Beck. You see, I also lost my—"

"Do find a place for Mrs. Beck's lovely dish," Mrs. Montrose told her maid, already leaving the dining room to return to her guests.

By the time I had watched her go, I turned back to find that Lupe-the-maid had cleared the perfect spot for my casserole dish. She reached for it, potholders and all, placed it down, and removed the lid. Steam swirled up from within it, and I sighed happily at the cheesy aroma. But as I looked around at the dining room, empty of people other than the two of us, I wondered if it would even get to be enjoyed while it was still warm.

Before I could thank her, Lupe had whisked the lid and potholders toward the kitchen, and as soon as I was left alone, I felt more than awkward. Why on earth had Pastor Jeff thought these people needed a casserole? And delivered by someone who was actually in mourning, no less?

I looked over the table, filled with shrimp rolls and zucchini parmesan and slices of triple-layer tuxedo cake, and tried to decide if I was hungry. The least I could get out of this task was a decent meal, and it wasn't as though anyone was around to see me help myself.

But I sighed and decided against it. Even if I thought I was hungry now, one or two bites in, and I'd realize I wasn't.

I headed back for the foyer. Not a single black-clad person looked my way as I slunk through the front room, not even Mrs. Montrose, whose cream-colored dress stood out against the sea of black. She was currently being jabbered at by a skinny man with dark slicked-back hair in a three-piece dark suit. As I passed, I heard him say, "We need to hire somebody ourselves, find the car that hit him, and sue the pants off the guy."

The man winked twice at Mrs. Montrose. At first, I thought he was trying to send her some kind of a secret signal like Marty Sims, the protagonist in Cooper's mystery series might have done, but after he did it again, I realized I'd only been reading too many of Cooper's novels. It was clearly a tic.

I moved through the open room toward the foyer with my mind still on mystery novels. I hadn't heard how the man of the house—Dan Montrose—had died, but from the sounds of things, it was an accident where the other driver had fled the scene. If it had been a murder, who would be the culprit? The maid in the short skirt? The radiant and beaming wife of the deceased? Or the mysterious man in the three-piece-suit who had a tic?

Maybe I wouldn't be so bad at concocting my own mysteries, after all. At the very least, I could entertain Cooper's cat.

Just inside the foyer, I stopped in place. A lady stood in my path. She wore a simple black skirt with a matching billowy blouse and stood facing away, holding a photograph of what must have been Dan Montrose. I could immediately tell by her shoes—a JC Penny black pump with scuffs on the heels—that she wasn't as wealthy as most of this crowd.

I didn't want to retreat into the open room of people, but I also couldn't get to my own pair of lone coral flats I'd kicked off without asking this lady to move. I figured that was the lesser of the two uncomfortable options and cleared my throat. The woman turned to reveal her tear-streaked, familiar face.

"Beth?" I asked at the same time she said, "Mallory Beck?"

Beth Dawson had been our realtor when Cooper and I looked for our first house in Honeysuckle Grove.

I looked again from the photo in her hands to Beth's tear-streaked face. "I'm so sorry," I said—the one phrase I swore I'd never say to a grieving person, as it didn't help one bit. I quickly covered with, "How did you know the, um, deceased?"

Beth nodded and placed the photo back onto the foyer's narrow oak table. "He was my sister's husband. It's just awful what happened."

"Oh? Your sister is Mrs. Montrose?" I could see the resemblance now. Beth wore her auburn hair closer to her head and donned a fair bit less makeup, although she clearly wore some, as it had streaked around her eyes.

"Yes, Helen is my sister," she said, and the statement seemed loaded with...something. Underlying emotion? Years of sisterly fights over shared clothes and competing for boys?

This thought made me immediately piece together the fact that Mrs. Helen Montrose seemed perfectly fine after her husband's very recent death—only five days ago—while her sister was quite broken up about it.

I had to comment. "It seems like your sister is holding herself together quite well."

Beth twisted her lips and tilted her head. I wasn't entirely sure what the look meant, but then she went on to say, "You know who's really hurting over Dan's death? The children. They haven't been eating, don't want to talk to me or to Helen, and haven't even come out of their rooms all day."

I put a hand to my chest, physically hurt from the thought of how much his children must be suffering. I glanced down at my lone pair of flats, which someone—probably Lupe—had aligned neatly beside a wooden coatrack. But now I didn't want to leave. Helen Montrose didn't want my help and comfort, but perhaps someone in this household did.

"Do you think it would be okay if I brought the kids a plate of food to their rooms?" I asked Beth. Being their aunt, she would know if this was inappropriate. "I just brought a fresh casserole."

Beth smiled. "You know, they'd probably love that. I think they're tired of everyone they know asking them if they're all right. I promised I'd give them their space today, but I hate knowing they're not getting anything to eat."

I smiled. "Where do I find their bedrooms?"

"Right up the stairs from the dining room. Come on, I'll show you."

Before she turned to lead the way, I said, "Wait," and dug into my purse for a tissue. I pulled one out of a package and handed it to her, motioning to her eyes.

She smiled her thanks, and a second later, Beth was tidied up and leading me back through the open room of people. Not a single person looked away from their conversations to us. Lupe wove around the room with a tray of canapés, which made it clear why the dining room was so deserted. Apparently, these people didn't retrieve their own food.

As we moved through to the dining room, I asked Beth, "I overheard something earlier, and, well...Was your brother-in-law killed in a car accident, a hit-and-run?"

Beth let out a long sigh. "That's what they tell us, yes. Where did you hear that?"

A rush of heat traveled up my neck for having been caught eavesdropping. "Oh, well, I had just been about to say goodbye to your sister, and a man was telling her he wanted to find the car who hit Dan and sue him, or something like that."

Beth nodded and slipped a tendril of shoulder-length auburn hair behind her ear. "That would be Terrence Lane. He's another lawyer at the firm where Dan was a partner." She shook her head. "I'd heard there wasn't much chance of finding the person responsible. If Terrence can, I'm all for it."

If the person took off, it seemed as though there had to be a way to find the person so he or she could at least be held accountable for that.

But Beth sighed again. "I supposed it wouldn't bring Dan back, regardless. This family has enough money, and I'm sure the person already feels awful.

So what's the point? Why not just let everyone get past their grief and move on with their lives."

She didn't ask it as a question, and so I didn't answer. I couldn't say I agreed with her. If Cooper's death hadn't so clearly been an accident, if there had been any mystery hanging over the fire at the bank, about why it had happened or who was at fault, I would not have been able to think about anything else.

Although, I guess that was true anyway.

"Oooh, that looks good," Beth said, taking my attention and pointing to my casserole. "Amber loves melted cheese."

I reached for one of the untouched plates and dug a heaping scoop out of the casserole dish. Then I decided I should really include a small mound of each type of pasta. It would mess up the appearance of the rest of the casserole, but it wasn't like that mattered too much in the empty dining room. "And Amber is the Montrose daughter, I assume?"

"Yes. She's fifteen and has been pretty upended about the whole thing."

"No doubt. Is she the oldest?"

Beth shook her head. "Danny Jr. Or I guess he's going by his middle name, Seth, lately. He's seventeen. He's been really angry. I don't know if he'd take any food, but you could try."

Her tone didn't sound hopeful, but nevertheless, I reached for another plate and filled it with an extra-large helping of pasta. I'd heard that teenage boys could eat. Soon I had two beautiful, appetizing tri-colored pasta plates ready for delivery.

"Right up there," Beth said, pointing up a set of stairs. "Danny's room is at the top of the stairs. Amber's is halfway along on the right."

"Okay, thanks. You're sure you don't want to come along?" Now that I was actually making a move toward the stairs, awkwardness consumed me. I didn't know these people, after all.

Beth lifted her flat palms up to face me. "No, no. I'm giving them their space. Oh, and I should warn you, if Danny's friend Cade is with him, you might just want to leave them be."

I was already on the second stair, but I turned back. "Yeah? Why's that?"

Beth shook her head as she headed for the kitchen. "When those two get together, they're never up to any good."

End of excerpt. Get the full novel now to read on!

Turn the page to travel to Crystal Cove for another Sneak Peek...

Sneak Peek - Witchy Wednesday (Book 1 in the Tabitha Chase Days of the Week Mysteries)

Chapter One

WHEN I WAS A little girl, my Auntie Lizzie told me there were two ways to get to Crystal Cove, Oregon—over the mountains on the interstate or the way she arrived: on a broomstick across the skies.

As an eight-year-old, I'd wanted to believe her stories with everything in me despite the forewarnings of my pragmatic parents. Through the years, and after many real-world obstacles, I'd come to the understanding that those stories were only the fodder of elaborate make-believe, told by people who chose to focus on the imaginary instead of looking head-on at their real-life problems. My learning had become complete a month ago when Aunt Lizzie left a note for her sister, my mom, and then jumped off Crystal Falls to her death.

Crystal Cove used to hold awe and mystique like Disneyland, but as I descended the 101 out of the Calapooya Mountains through rain so slick I could barely see the front of my car, going to take care of some postmortem details, I decided the last tiny part of me that believed in magic had officially died with my aunt.

My windshield wipers squeaked at regular intervals, and my old Honda smelled awful with exhaust, having worked harder than she had in a long time to get up and through the mountain passes. My hands were white-knuckle-locked onto my steering wheel, and I'd been squinting at the road in front of me for almost three hours. This road demanded a lot more than autopilot, but I jumped in my seat when my phone rang through the Bluetooth, letting me know I'd better clue back in.

I fumbled over my phone, not looking away from the road for even a second, and answered, "Hi, Dad. I'm almost there."

The pause that followed made me glance down at my phone screen for one quick heartbeat. Shoot. I'd done it again.

It wasn't my dad, who knew all about my trip to Crystal Cove and had pretty much forced it upon me. Nope. It was my boss, Brendan Reiger, who had yet to hear about my impromptu trip and who I had planned to explain it to much more delicately as soon as I had the chance.

"Almost . . . where, Tabitha?" Brendan said through my car's speakers. He had a deep, almost ominous voice. All the realtors in our Portland office thought it was the authority that came with that kind of voice that helped him make so many quick sales. We joked about how his prospective clients were likely scared for their lives if they didn't sign on the dotted line exactly when he told them to. His voice sounded even deeper tonight, which made me momentarily forget my strategic wording and blurt out the truth.

"Oh, yes, well, I just had to take a quick trip down the coast. I, um, I had a death in the family." I hoped he wouldn't ask how recent the death was. I suspected if I had to explain that Aunt Lizzie died almost a month ago, he'd lack the bit of sympathy I had hoped to garner from my tough-as-nails boss.

Instead, he said, "Oh. Who died?"

I blinked hard, trying to split my attention between the rain-soaked road and this phone call. I really should have pulled over—if only I could see the shoulder. "It was my Aunt Lizzie." My voice came out more full of drama than I intended, which only made Brendan pry more.

"Right. Were you close, then?"

I couldn't, in good conscience, say yes. I hadn't seen my aunt in years. But instead I searched for something that might seem like the affirmative. "She was my mom's little sister." Again with the drama, Tabby? Take some acting lessons already!

"And you'll be back tomorrow? We have that showing in Stafford and I hoped I could count on you for putting up signage."

Putting up signage. Was that what my job had become? I'd been giving the Portland real estate market all I had for the past three years. I spent late nights and early mornings drafting market reports, researching amenities, and perfecting my staging skills. At every turn, Brendan suggested I'd be his next superstar realtor, but then he'd saddle me with staging rundown townhouses, blowing up balloons for open houses, and now putting up signage.

"Um, it's a long drive," I said as I passed a weathered wooden sign with faded paint boasting: WELCOME TO CRYSTAL COVE. The road was shrouded with trees on either side, and my GPS showed a few miles yet before I'd reach the town center and then the marina. There were no streetlights out this far, and I continued to squint to see through the rain as I mentally berated myself for picking up the call. "So I probably won't make it back by tomorrow."

"By Tuesday then." It didn't sound like a question. When I didn't say anything right away, he went on. "Our office has been talking to a client from Forest Park. I think they're ready to list, and wouldn't that be the perfect neighborhood for your first solo listing? Wouldn't that make your dad proud?"

My heart rate sped up, both from the idea of my own listing, in Forest Park no less, and from the idea of my father being proud. He was a state senator, and with his endless connections, he'd offered to get me a job with a local realtor as soon as I'd passed the exam, but I'd refused, wanting to prove myself and make my own way in the real estate world. More than once, I'd regretted that quick decision, but now I slowly let a breath seep out of me. Maybe it was time to finally see some fruits from my labor.

I'd barely let out my breath when an obstruction in the middle of the road made me slam on my brakes. I shrieked as the form of a woman came into view.

She was lying right in the middle of the rain-soaked road.

"Tabitha?" Brendan asked. "I can count on you to be back on Tuesday, right?"

"I—uh—I have to go." I couldn't tune into Brendan's reply as I slammed my car into PARK, grabbed for my phone, and got out of my car. I left it running, with the windshield wipers working furiously to keep up with the rain and the headlights aimed toward the woman. As I moved closer and pulled the hood of my jacket up over my head, she appeared dead—face up but with one of her jean-clad legs out at an odd angle—spread almost to the splits and bent upward at the knee, which was clearly broken. The odd angles of this woman's body in the midst of the brutal storm with the narrow lighting of my headlights made me momentarily see the situation as a meticulously planned horror movie. I blinked and then shook my head, reminding myself this was real.

"Hello? Hello? Are you okay?" I called. My heart rate ratcheted up as I moved closer and looked into her unblinking eyes. She had striking features—red full lips and thick eyelashes. She looked so alive. My phone was still in my hand, getting soaked, so I tucked it under my jacket and dialed 911.

A second later, a woman answered. "911. What is your emergency?"

"There's a woman. In the middle of the road. I don't think she's breathing."

The operator asked me for my location, and I tried to think as I bent closer to the woman. She wore a bright yellow poncho that looked hand-knit. It immediately made me wonder who had knit it for her—who would be devastated by the news of her passing. "Um. Off highway 101. Just past the welcome sign to Crystal Cove."

I reached for the woman's wrist as the operator confirmed my location. Fresh out of college, I'd attempted a short career as a personal trainer. I'd taken a fitness first aid course, but it felt like a million years ago. Still, training or no training, I knew not finding a pulse was bad news. I explained this to the operator. She instructed me to wait where I was and an emergency vehicle would arrive as soon as possible. After hanging up, I reached for the woman's neck. She was still warm, but I couldn't find a pulse there either. When I pulled my hand away, it was covered in rain mixed with blood.

The metallic scent hit my nose and I gagged. I'd never been great with the sight or smell of blood, and in an instant, I was up and backed against the hood of my car, trying to keep my dinner from three hours ago down in my stomach where it belonged. I kept my eyes from my bloodied hand for long enough that I could catch my breath and hoped the rain would wash the bulk of the blood off before I had to look at it. But the sky chose this moment to close up and stop its torrential downpour.

"Great, the one time I actually want the rain," I murmured toward the sky. My windshield wipers squeaked against the drying glass as I moved back toward my driver's door and found a napkin in the door storage with my left hand while holding my right hand as far as possible away from my nose. I flicked off the wipers, then I held my breath as I wiped off the blood and looked around for somewhere I could dispose of the dirtied napkin.

Never usually one to litter, I couldn't help myself tonight. I tossed it into the roadside bushes. The metallic smell was still playing awful tricks on my stomach. I bent to douse my hand in a nearby puddle as sirens sounded in the distance. My headlights caught something blue and gleaming right beside the puddle.

I picked up what I'd thought was a shiny rock, but it looked more like a tiny jewel once I had it in my hand. I studied the jagged surface. It was smaller than my pinkie nail and probably wasn't worth anything, but it seemed like glass, maybe that sea glass my aunt used to tell me about, and so I tucked it into my jacket pocket and stood as the sirens grew louder and I tried to collect myself.

I walked a wide circle around the woman on the ground, taking note of any details that might be helpful for the ambulance upon its arrival. On her front side, the woman appeared soaked from the rain but otherwise unmarked. Her hair was a strawberry blonde, less red than mine but still red enough to make out the hue even while soaking wet and lit only by my headlights. Now that the rain had subsided, the blood on her neck was visible. Her eyes remained eerily open, looking up at the sky as though she might be waiting to be taken up to heaven.

A firetruck arrived on scene first. It parked at an angle, blocking half the road, and two burly firemen emerged from the front doors.

A third fireman came around from the back of the truck and headed straight for me. "Are you all right? What happened here? Are you injured?"

"No, I'm fine. I didn't hit the woman. She was like this when I arrived." I'd been leaning over to see if I could find anything else of this woman's injuries, but as the fireman moved between me and the woman, I didn't hesitate to take several large steps back.

One of the other firemen quickly set up a large work light, illuminating several feet in all directions of the woman.

"And your name?" the first fireman asked me. He had a square jaw and was clean-shaven, unlike his two coworkers.

"Tabitha . . ." I hesitated, as my father had drilled into me about a thousand times to keep the Chase name as quiet as possible on this trip. But the fireman kept staring at me, a pen poised over his notepad, so I had no choice but to add, "Chase. Tabitha Chase."

Before the fireman could ask me anything more, a dark sedan with blue and red flashing lights and its siren screaming whipped around the corner and parked sideways, blocking the road behind my car. The firetruck blocked most of the road in the other direction, which left all five of us, plus the woman's body, in a small cocoon of space.

A man in a suit, I guessed him to be a detective, emerged from the dark sedan, came around my car, and set his dark eyes squarely on the unshaven fireman.

"Tell me what we've got here, Tucker." It sounded more like an order than a question.

"Just arrived on scene, sir."

"Looks like posterior injuries," one of the bearded firemen called out from where he was bent near the woman.

"She's bleeding on the back of her neck," I volunteered helpfully.

The detective's head snapped toward me. "Did you move this woman?"

I shook my head. "No, of course not. I just checked for a pulse."

The detective's brow furrowed, like he wasn't sure he believed me. He also reached to check for a pulse but on her wrist. "Is this the exact placement the woman fell to?" He stood again and loomed over me.

"I—I guess so."

His eyes drilled into me, waiting for more. "Did you move her legs?"

"No! I mean, I just found her like this."

Again with the furrowed brow. "You didn't hit her with your vehicle?"

"No, she was already here," I said again.

"No pulse. Posterior trauma," the clean-shaven fireman said, still making notes. "Mick should be here soon."

The detective nodded and yelled at one of the bearded firemen, who was tilting up the woman's body to have a look at her back. "Are you kidding me, Johnson? Don't move her!" He turned back to the clean-shaven fireman—Tucker—who seemed to be in charge of the firetruck contingent. "She was struck down?" He flipped open his own notebook and started scribbling notes before Tucker had started to answer.

"Well, no, Tom." I found it interesting that the bully of a detective seemed to bark at everyone by their last names, and yet this Fireman Tucker called the detective Tom. "Or I don't know. No pulse, only posterior injuries. But this lady, Tabitha Chase, says she was like this when she arrived." Tucker motioned to me, and the detective turned and set eyes solidly on me for the first time. Or, at least, he set eyes on my brown leather boots. It took about three long seconds for his eyes to travel up the rest of me to my face.

I was an awful mess—soaked through my brown wool coat and even through my sweater. My normally orangey-red hair felt slick against my forehead, and I most certainly didn't feel like being ogled. "Yes, she was like this when I found her," I said for the third time, almost feeling doubt in myself for all the skeptical looks being thrown my way. "It was raining like crazy. I'm just glad I saw her in time to stop and call 911."

"In time?" Tom the detective raised his dark eyebrows at me.

I swallowed, the seriousness of the situation hitting me anew. Because I hadn't seen the woman in time. "I meant in time to stop. So I didn't run over her." My voice dropped, and I bowed my head, belatedly trying to show some respect.

"You got an identity yet?" Tom the detective barked toward the three firemen. He didn't wait for an answer and moved closer to the woman. "Ah.

The Doerksen woman. Another one of those witches."

My head snapped up. "Witches?" I couldn't help but ask. My aunt had told fortunes for a living, so it wasn't as if I was completely unfamiliar with the word. It just seemed so strange, hearing it out of the all-business detective's mouth.

Tom snapped his look back to me. "Do you know this woman?"

I shook my head without looking at her. "I'm not even from here."

"So you've never met Maple May Doerksen?" Tom asked again. Why didn't anyone in this town believe me? It wasn't as though I was the one who'd been a fortune-teller in this town for over twenty years, charging people money to make up stories for them!

"I've never met Maple May Doerksen," I said, deadpan.

Before Tom the detective could question me further, a light-colored sedan arrived. It parked in the small gap of road left unoccupied by the firetruck and the detective's sedan, and that's when I noticed the lineup of lights down the road in the darkness. Traffic, it seemed, had accumulated, but unlike in the city where people would be honking their horns by now, people had gotten out of their vehicles and stood in a group at a distance, whispering about the scene in front of them.

The man in the light sedan was the "Mick" they had been waiting for. Mick wore a white lab coat and studied the body on the road while the detective stood nearby, updating him with everything he'd heard from me and Fireman Tucker.

It seemed as though everyone had forgotten about me. When I shivered again from the cold seeping through to my skin, I sidled up beside the bearded fireman who had returned to his truck. "Excuse me? Do you think it's all right if I go now?"

He took one glance over my shoulder at my car. "Don't think you'd be able to, even if it was okay."

I turned and saw what he meant. Not only was my car blocked by the detective's sedan, but now there were a half dozen vehicles lined up behind that.

I nodded my thanks and headed back to my car. The engine was still running, burning a lot of gas, and my headlights were still on. I got into my driver's seat, turned off my headlights, and cranked up my heat. The firemen had set up three portable lights by this time, so I didn't think the absence of my headlights would make any difference, but the moment they flicked off, Tom's gaze snapped to my car and he marched straight over.

I unrolled my window as he said, "Where do you think you're going?"

I clearly wasn't going anywhere, but his tone made me angry. "I'm warming up! I'm soaked right through all my clothes, and you gave me no idea how long I might be here, so I had no choice but to take care of myself."

Tom the detective nodded. "Take care of yourself." Again, his words made me feel like I was responsible for this horrible accident. He didn't stay to accuse me of anything outright, though. Instead, he strode to the front of my car, squatted, and started studying it with a flashlight.

This guy was too much.

Cold or not, I buttoned up my coat and got out of my car. I stomped around to the front. "Look, I told you I didn't hit that lady with my car. I've told you and your firemen three times, and I have no idea why you keep—"

He stood and got right in my face. "Well, if you didn't run into Maple May, why is there blood on your hood? Would you like to tell me that?" He shone the flashlight at my light blue Honda Civic, and sure enough, there was a streak of dark red across the front edge of the hood. "I'll bet you a million dollars if we test it, it'll match up with Maple May's blood."

My mind scrambled for an answer as I burned with anger. Had I hit the woman and knocked my head and forgotten the whole thing? Was I completely delusional? But then my answer burst out of my mouth the second it came to me. "That was from me! My hand." Tom tried to interrupt, but I didn't let him. "I'd tried to take the woman's pulse . . . while I was on the line with 911. My hand got blood on it, and I wiped it—"

"You wiped it on your car?" He raised an unbelieving eyebrow at me.

I waved toward the bushes. "No, Tom." If he was going to talk to me like I was stupid, I was determined to do the same right back to him. "I wiped it on a napkin, but I guess I got some on my car. Yes, it will match that woman's blood, but no, I absolutely did not hit her with my car!"

Tom took his flashlight toward the bushes. When he located the offending napkin, he pulled out a small plastic Ziploc with the word "Evidence" emblazoned on the side. I resisted the urge to roll my eyes. After all, if these people still chose to believe I had hit the woman with my car, I didn't have a lot of ways to prove otherwise.

After that, Tom took a swab of "evidence" from the front hood of my car. He turned to me when he was done. "I'll need your driver's license and registration, please, ma'am." I bent into my car to retrieve them but not before he spoke his next words to me. "And I'd also love an explanation for why you think it's appropriate to call me Tom."

Chapter Two

I stared at the detective for a long moment with my driver's license in one hand and my insurance papers in the other. Sure, I was angry, but getting on this detective's bad side before I'd even made it into Crystal Cove seemed like the last thing I should do.

"I didn't mean to be disrespectful. I just heard Mr. Tucker over there call you Tom."

The detective cleared his throat. "It's Detective Thom. T-H-O-M." Before I had a chance to respond, he snatched my license and papers from my hands and, without another word, strode purposefully back to his car with them.

What a jerk! I was in no hurry to talk to Detective Thom again, but he returned what seemed like seconds later.

"Where were you planning on going from here, Miss Chase? I see you live in Portland."

I nodded once. "I'm headed into Crystal Cove for a short time. A day or two at most."

The detective studied my face for a long moment before he spoke. "I'll need a phone number and address for where you'll be staying here in town."

I gave him my cell number and the address for the marina where my aunt's houseboat was docked. I wasn't sure if Aunt Lizzie's boat was going to be the most comfortable place for me to stay. I hadn't slept on her couch since I was eight, but I figured I could always find a nearby hotel tomorrow.

"Which boat?" Detective Thom asked.

"I—uh—" Suddenly, I was certain he'd know exactly who my Aunt Lizzie had been, and that was the last thing I needed at the scene of the death of a local witch. But it seemed I had no choice. "Um . . . the Lady of Fortune?" I asked it as a question, even though I'd known the silly name for my aunt's boat since I could talk.

The detective looked back at my license before handing it back over. "The Lady of Fortune?" His tone seemed too light for the moment or this information. "And can you tell me who you plan to visit there?"

He was playing with me, trying to trap me. I could feel it. My dad had told me to keep quiet in town about my relationship with Aunt Lizzie. The last thing he needed for his campaign was a connection to a recent suicide. But this was different. This was the police, and I clearly needed to come clean with the whole truth if I was ever going to get out from under Detective Thom's suspicion.

"Lizzie Rose was my aunt," I told him. "I'm here to clean up her houseboat and get it up for sale. That's all."

His eyes moved side to side over mine for a few seconds, as if he were trying to read any lies. I kept mine squarely locked on his.

But before he could respond, Mick in the white lab coat called him over. "Hey, Thom. Come and look at this."

I waited and watched while they had a quiet conversation over the dead woman's body. I'd never seen a dead person in real life, and the more I looked at Maple May Doerksen, the more it seemed unbelievable that she wouldn't simply sit up and start talking again. How could she truly be dead? And so instantly? I looked again around the scene, now blocked in by emergency vehicles and lit like a movie set.

I couldn't hear much of what Detective Thom or the medical examiner were saying, but when the detective left the man in white, he told him, "I'll likely have to get Jameson in on this one." Then he returned to me and instructed me to wait in my car until he had a chance to clear the traffic and make a path for me to get out. He passed me a business card. "And I'd appreciate it if you'd let me know before you leave town, in case we have any further questions."

I took his card, agreed, and got back into my now-cold vehicle. Even once I had it idling and pumping out the heat full blast, I couldn't seem to warm up.

I'd seen a dead body tonight.

I'd almost run her over.

And worst of all, Detective Thom had accused me of killing her.

If I believed in bad omens, that would most definitely be what the start of this trip felt like.

Chapter Three

It was after midnight by the time I found the Crystal Beach Marina. It wasn't very well lit, and I didn't have much in the way of memories of which boat was my aunt's. Had I known I would arrive this late, I definitely would have booked a hotel.

I sighed and got out of my car, thankful that the rain was continuing to hold off for the moment. I'd brought a small wheeling suitcase with my overnight things, and it clacked and bumped over the wooden slats of the wharf as I followed my mom's written directions to where I'd find the Lady of Fortune. I had no idea if others lived on boats here and if I might be clacking by anyone's beds, but I was too exhausted to care enough to pick up my suitcase.

I passed a few small sailboats that didn't look large enough to have inhabitants and then made a left toward the bigger boats. When the first fancy yacht came into view, I couldn't help myself and hoisted my suitcase up by its handle with a grunt. Everything seemed silent, aside from the waves lapping at the sides of the wharf. There were only three large motorized yachts in a line before I came to the houseboats.

As a child, I'd had a romanticized view of living on a houseboat, but as I passed each of the dilapidated structures now, trying to recognize my aunt's, my realtor's brain kicked in, and even in the dark, I noticed water abrasions and could immediately name a dozen bits that needed sprucing up.

But if I thought the bits and pieces of wear on the first couple of houseboats were bad, that was nothing compared to when I finally came to the boat labeled "ady of F tune" in the final slip on this wharf.

A wash of memories overtook me as I stared up at the multi-colored flags strung from mast to tip, the purple curtains flounced under the second-story overhang, and the wrought iron furniture on the front deck. When I was an eight-year-old, this boat had felt like an attraction at a theme park, but now that I was as an adult, and even in the dark, the large structure didn't look like something I wanted to climb aboard. The rusty old vessel looked like more of a sailboat or even a tugboat than a boxy houseboat. The other ones in the line seemed more like real houses—part of the real estate market—simply balancing on the water, but my aunt's boat looked as though it had once been sea-worthy—though I would not trust it outside of the harbor now.

I looked again to the wrought iron table and chairs, now rusty, and purple bejeweled drapes, trying to remember if that was where my aunt had done her fortune-telling.

The rear of the boat had two stories of interior space, but the only door to get inside was via the front deck. I held a rail on the boat as I stepped across the short gangplank that joined it to the wharf and immediately felt my legs wobble from the transition. Once fully aboard the boat, I took a couple of seconds to let my body adjust to the regular movement from the waves. Then I headed for the door and rustled the key my mom had given me out by the time I made my way under the purple curtains.

At first, the key didn't turn at all. In a panic, I jiggled it and pushed the door with my shoulder at the same time, and thankfully it started to give way. With a little more force, it eventually nudged open. Silence greeted me. It didn't feel like the safest place to stay by myself at night. In fact, it seemed as though there was no one else around the entire marina.

But the idea of leaving and finding a hotel tonight exhausted me, and even the thought brought my eyes to half-mast.

"I'll fix the doorknob first thing tomorrow," I murmured to myself, pushing the rest of the way through the door and then using my phone's flashlight to look around a bigger space than I remembered.

I'd visited my aunt a handful of times when I was little, usually for long weekends when my parents took an adults-only vacation to Wine Country, California. My brother and sister always chose to stay back in Portland with friends, but my first choice had always been Aunt Lizzie's. The last time I'd been here, I'd gone home with stories of magic spells and spiritual eyesight, and my parents had decided she wasn't a great influence on me. After that, my mom started to visit her half-sister a few times a year on her own, and my parents hired a sitter to stay with us in Portland when they went away.

The interior of the boat brought more memories: the sea air, mixed with a hint of mildew. That ever-present motion that made you feel a mix of unsteady and peacefully rocked. The homey warm orange colors decorating the loveseat and chairs and even some braided artwork on the walls. My dad had spoken of the boat as a commodity so many times in the last month that I'd momentarily formed a clinical picture in my head. Now my aunt's spiritedness came flooding back in every inch of what had been her home.

This was also fortune-telling-central. That was clear by the wooden table with a chair on either side, flouncing purple-and-orange tablecloth with beaded tassels, and a crystal ball on a thick wooden base, right at the center of the table.

I'd yet to find a light switch in this boat, and when my phone light went dim and a second later something rubbed up against my chins, I nearly came out of my skin.

I shrieked and jumped away in one motion. Fumbling over my phone, I eventually got the lights turned back on in time to see what I initially thought was a small raccoon that had followed me onto the boat. But after only a second of my eyes adjusting, I saw instead a cat with legs so short, its belly hung almost to the floor.

"Shoo! Shoo!" I told it, waving my free hand. My parents had never had any pets—Mom was physically allergic, while Dad was emotionally allergic—and so I didn't have a high comfort level around cats, dogs, hamsters, or even fish. What I knew about stray cats came from TV and included sharp claws, urine spraying, and rabies.

But the squat gray striped cat didn't listen and instead skirted right between my legs and deeper into the boat.

"Hey, come back here!" My voice gave away my utter exhaustion, and when I shone my flashlight around the entire space and couldn't locate the cat, I decided that would just be one more thing I had to put out of my mind if I was going to get any sleep at all tonight. There was so much work to be done on this boat before selling it—what would be the difference if I had to clean up a little cat pee?

At least in the process of trying to find the cat, I located the door to the upper deck and my aunt's bedroom.

I figured I'd had enough bad fortune for one day. The universe must be able to see that.

End of excerpt. Get the full book now to read on!

Turn the page for a couple of Mallory and Tabby's favorite recipes!

Recipe: Blueberry Buckle Coffee Cake

THIS IS ONE OF Mallory's favorite recipes from culinary school. It's easy to make, moist, and full of juicy berries. Use fresh berries in the summer or frozen ones in the winter.

Ingredients:

Streusel:

1/3 cup granulated sugar

1/2 cup Unbleached All-Purpose Flour

1 teaspoon cinnamon

1/8 teaspoon salt

4 tablespoons butter, at room temperature

Cake:

2 cups Unbleached All-Purpose Flour

2 teaspoons baking powder

1/2 teaspoon salt

3/4 cup granulated sugar

4 tablespoons butter, softened

1 large egg, at room temperature

1 teaspoon Vanilla Extract

1/2 cup milk, at room temperature

2 cups blueberries, fresh or frozen

Instructions:

Preheat the oven to 375°F. Lightly grease a 9" square cake pan.

To make the streusel topping: In a small bowl, mix the sugar, flour, cinnamon, and salt. Cut in the butter with two knives until it reaches a crumbly state. Set aside.

To make the cake: In a medium-sized mixing bowl, whisk together the flour, baking powder, and salt.

In a separate bowl, beat together the sugar, butter, egg, and vanilla.

Alternately add the milk and the flour mixture to the sugar/butter mixture, ending with flour. Add blueberries. Stir just enough to blend.

Pour the batter into the prepared pan. Sprinkle the streusel topping over the batter.

Bake for 40 to 45 minutes, or until a toothpick inserted into the center comes out clean.

Remove the cake from the oven, and set it on a rack to cool for 10 minutes. Serve right from the pan and enjoy!

Recipe: Christmassy Peppermint Mocha

INGREDIENTS:

3/4 cup whole milk

3 tablespoons sugar

1 tablespoon unsweetened cocoa powder

3/4 cup brewed espresso or strong coffee

½ peppermint candy cane

1/4 teaspoon vanilla extract

whipped cream and chocolate shavings or crumbled candy cane

Instructions:

In a small saucepan, add milk, cocoa and sugar. Heat over medium heat until small bubbles begin to form around the edge and sugar has dissolved.

Stir in espresso, candy cane, and vanilla and remove from heat as soon as candy cane is melted completely.

Serve in a large mug and top with whipped cream and chocolate shavings or crumbled candy cane if desired.

Join My Cozy Mystery Readers' Newsletter Today!

Would you like to be among the first to hear about new releases and sales, and receive special excerpts and behind-the-scene bonuses?

Sign up now to get your free copy of Mystery of the Holiday Hustle – A Mallory Beck Cozy Holiday Mystery.

You'll also get access to special epilogues to accompany this series—an exclusive bonus for newsletter subscribers. Sign up below and receive your free mystery:

https://www.subscribepage.com/mysteryreaders

Would you like to be among the first to read new mysteries as they are being written? Would you enjoy voting on new character names as they are being introduced to the series? Would you like to see your name in the acknowledgments of a new book? If so, check out Denise's community at ReamStories.com/cozymysteries

Buy all of Denise's cozy mysteries direct from the author at shop.denisejaden.com for early access to new releases, deep discounts on book bundles, and fun clothing and collectibles to accompany the series'!

The Tabitha Chase Days of the Week Mysteries Book Order

Book 1 - Witchy Wednesday
Book 2 - Thrilling Thursday
Book 3 – Frightful Friday
Book 4 – Slippery Saturday
Book 5 – Sinister Sunday
Book 6 – Morbid Monday
Book 7 – Tragic Tuesday

Standalone Short Mystery –
Dead-end Weekend

The Mallory Beck Cozy Culinary Capers Book Order:

Book 1 – Murder at Mile Marker 18
Book 2 – Murder at the Church Picnic
Book 3 – Murder at the Town Hall
Book 4 – Murder in the Vineyard
Book 5 – Murder at the Montrose Mansion
Book 6 – Murder during the Antique Auction
Book 7 – Murder in the Secret Cold Case
Book 8 – Murder in New Orleans
Standalone Short Mystery –

Dead-end Weekend
Mystery of the Holiday Hustle –
Prequel Mystery

Collaborative Works:

Murder on the Boardwalk
Murder on Location
Saving Heart & Home

Nonfiction for Writers:

Writing with a Heavy Heart
Story Sparks
Fast Fiction

Denise Jaden is the author of the Mallory Beck Cozy Culinary Capers and the Tabitha Chase Days of the Week Mysteries. She is also the author of several critically-acclaimed young adult novels, and nonfiction books for writers, including the NaNoWriMo-popular guide Fast Fiction.

In her spare time, Denise acts in TV and movies and dances with a Polynesian dance troupe. She lives just outside Vancouver, British Columbia, with her husband, son, and one very spoiled cat.

Sign up on Denise's website to receive bonus content (you'll find clues in every bonus epilogue!) as well as updates on her new Cozy Mystery Series.

www.denisejaden.com

Acknowledgements

I'M SO GRATEFUL FOR my editor, Louise Bates, and my first reader, Monica Cobine. Their feedback helps my mysteries make sense and (hopefully) keeps them engaging. Big thanks also to my proofreaders Alan and Lynn, and to Chad, Mona, Tony, Dorothy, Merry, Lucia, Sheila, and one of my readers who goes by the name Mr. Wonderful--as well as the rest of my ARC team, who are wonderfully encouraging and great in helping to get the word out about my new books.

And thank you, reader, for picking up this book. I love telling stories and crafting mysteries, and I'm grateful to have found readers who enjoy them. I hope you will continue to visit Tabby and Sherlock in Crystal Cove, as well as Mallory and Hunch in Honeysuckle Grove, for many stories to come.